Unlucky
for
Some

13 Tales with a Bite
for Vengeful Hearts!

Also by Julia Edwards:

The Scar Gatherer series
The Leopard in the Golden Cage
Saving the Unicorn's Horn
The Falconer's Quarry
The Demon in the Embers
Slaves for the Isabella
The Shimmer on the Glass
The Ring from the Ruins

For adults
Time was Away

Julia Edwards

Unlucky
for
Some

Illustrated by Evgenia Malina

Published in the United Kingdom by:

Laverstock Publishing
129 Church Road, Laverstock, Salisbury,
Wiltshire, SP1 1RB, UK

Text copyright © Julia Edwards, 2021
Illustrations © Evgenia Malina, 2021

First printed October 2021
ISBN: 978-1-9169027-1-8

www.juliaedwardsbooks.com
www.evgeniamalina.com

For Tom

Thank yous

This is the bit of the book most people skip over, where I admit to all the help I had writing this collection!

My husband started me off by suggesting I write something for fun, which this collection really was! My sons' honest reactions told me clear as day when a story wasn't working – one of these went through four endings before I got it right. I also tried the collection out on my parents, and it's down to my dad that Fur Elise finishes the way it does – if you met him, you'd never guess he was that nasty.

Most of all, though, I owe huge thanks to Clare Dallard and Amanda Hodgson and their Year Five and Six classes at St. Andrew's Primary School in Salisbury for being such enthusiastic guinea pigs. They laughed, gasped and groaned in all the right places, and we had a lot of fun together.

I hope you do too. I always think there's nothing like a bit of pure, vindictive enjoyment!

Contents

Fur Elise

I never liked Elise, not from the first moment I set eyes on her, even though I had no idea of the truth about her.

It didn't help that she was a girl – I don't have much to do with girls these days. I used to play with them back when I was in Infants. Never her though. Now I'm in Year Five, our class is pretty much divided, boys v. girls. Some of the girls are okay, I suppose. There certainly isn't anyone else as annoying as Elise.

Elise was one of those girls who wear stupid big bows in their hair, and suck up to the teacher all day long. "Of course, Miss March. Can I take that to the office for you, Miss March? Would you like me to lick your face clean, Miss March?"

I couldn't stand her! Sometimes, I'd daydream about strangling her, especially when she was book-monitor for the week. She'd make such a thing about giving the books out! "Here you are, Mo!" she'd say. "Here's your book for you!" And she'd give me that sugary smile that made me want to slap her!

I had a feeling Miss March couldn't stand her either. Maybe that was why she gave Elise the class hamster to take home for the Easter holidays. You see, it wasn't the treat it is in some schools, or even in other classes in our school. You really didn't want to be the one who had to look after our class pet, because Rookie was a vicious little git!

Miss March said hamsters are nocturnal, which makes you wonder why a school would get one, since nobody's even in the building at night. I don't suppose Rookie cared, though. He probably loved spinning round crazily in his wheel while we were all safely out of the way. I imagined him with glowing red eyes, scheming to take over the world as he went round and round.

All day long, of course, he'd be asleep inside the little plastic house in his cage, not even visible. If you tried to get him out, if you even just poked around with your finger to check he was there, he'd bite you. I don't mean a nibble either! He gave Tariq a full-on razor-fanged chomp when he put his hand in.

It was stupid of Tariq, really. He should have known

better than to listen to Daniel telling him Rookie was just a cuddly little fluff-ball. Surely he knew that nobody contradicts Daniel! That was why nobody said anything. Daniel totally knew what a evil little fiend Rookie was, of course, but he's as vicious as the hamster! He thought it was hilarious that Tariq had to go off to the hospital to get his finger stitched up and have some jabs!

So anyway, I wasn't sure Elise actually wanted to take

Rookie home for the holidays. Lola said she'd heard her asking Miss March, but I didn't believe it at the time. I mean, why would you volunteer to look after an animal that would like nothing better than to take your hand off? Afterwards, I realised Lola had been telling the truth. Elise knew exactly what she was doing.

It was a Friday, and own clothes day for the end of term. Elise was wearing this prissy sort of fairy dress. I mean, really! She's ten, or will be quite soon. Hasn't she realised that fairy outfits are for little kids? I wasn't the only one who thought she looked stupid: Ewan said so, really loudly. She pretended not to hear him. It seems so weird, looking back – the two different sides of her character were so totally different. At the time, though, I didn't know there was another side. I thought this was just Elise just being her usual, annoying self, swishing her skirts and flicking her hair around, wanting everyone to look at her.

Unfortunately, we live on the same street as her family, and my mum would never listen when I told her what Elise was like. She thought that because she liked Elise's mum, us kids would automatically get on. Every time I tried to explain, she'd say I was being narrow-minded. The fact that Elise's family is English and we're Asian doesn't mean anything, she'd say. As though that had anything to do with it!

Elise's house is diagonally opposite ours, but

fortunately my bedroom's at the back, so I can't see into her room from my window. Imagine that! I might have seen her tying the awful bow in her hair! Or something much worse, I realise now.

Elise's mum picked her up by car on that Friday, because of the hamster cage and all the food and everything, and she offered to give me a lift home. Elise's mum is as bad as mine for thinking we're bound to be friends – I guess she can't imagine someone not adoring her darling daughter! I said no thanks, I was happy to walk, and made something up about stopping off at a friend's house because Elise's mum wasn't going to take no for an answer.

It turned out, though, they hadn't collected everything from school for Rookie, because at about seven o'clock that evening, Elise's mum messaged my mum to ask if we had one of those water bottles that fixes onto the side of the cage. It seemed that Little Miss Perfect had forgotten to pack it. Did she forget though? I keep wondering that. Or did she just not bother? She bothered with the food, but I guess it would have been a bit obvious if she hadn't taken that.

We do have one of those bottles, as it happens, left over from when my brother used to keep gerbils, before he moved on to breeding scorpions to sell on the internet! Mum went and found it and gave it to me to take over the road. I started to ask why Elise couldn't come and get it – it was her mistake, after all – but I saw that glint in Mum's eye which means it's best to shut up. I took the bottle over to Elise's house and rang the doorbell, praying it wouldn't be her who opened the door.

It wasn't. It was her dad. He looked a bit vague. I explained why I'd come and he told me to go on up to Elise's room where they'd set up the cage. That was even worse than if she'd answered the front door herself! I was pretty desperate not to see her, especially not to go into her bedroom, but her dad just disappeared off down the hall.

I thought it would seem rude if I didn't do as he'd said, so I went slowly up the stairs, I was sort of hoping, I guess, that someone else in the family would come past and take the bottle from me. Nobody did.

I must have been quite quiet, I suppose, though not on purpose. Elise's dad had told me which room it was, and the door was slightly open. I peered through the gap. I wasn't spying – I just wanted to know what she was doing before I walked in on her.

Rookie's cage was on the other side of the room from the door, and I noticed the lid was open. Elise was standing in front of it, with her back to me. The way her arm was moving, and the little clicking noises, I guessed she was cutting something up, maybe a carrot for Rookie. I waited. I know it was mean, but I wanted to see her put her hand in the cage to feed him. It would be so funny to watch her get savaged! I didn't think it was very likely, mind you. Since Tariq, the whole class knew what Rookie was like. Besides, the hamster was probably asleep and wouldn't come out.

After a bit, it occurred to me that Elise had spent quite a long time doing whatever she was doing. Her head was bent over the table, like she was concentrating, and now and then, her left hand moved upwards. I edged into the gap and nudged the door with my toe. It was quiet in the room – she seemed to have mostly finished the cutting up – but I thought I could hear a crunching sound. Maybe Rookie was awake and had started on the carrot. Only there was something about the noise that wasn't quite right.

I nudged the door a bit wider, and this time it creaked. In the split second before Elise whipped round, I realised what was wrong with the crunching sound. It wasn't coming from the cage. It was coming from higher up.

Elise's jaws were still moving as she spun to face me. I'd been right about her cutting something up. The knife was still in her hand. Its long, sharp blade had something red on it. The fingers of her left hand were red too, and wet.

Worst of all was what was at the corner of her mouth.

Fur.

I dropped the bottle and ran.

Rookie had got out and vanished, she said, when she brought the empty cage to school on the first Monday back. She managed to cry when she told Miss March. She felt so bad, she said. Poor little hamster, stuck under the floorboards all on his own, wasting away with nothing to eat! Her parents had turned the place upside down apparently, but they couldn't find him. That bit was probably true, of course. They'd believed her just like Miss March believed her. I mean, you would, wouldn't you?

While Miss March talked to the class about Rookie's disappearance, in a serious voice that didn't quite hide her relief, I looked at Elise. She was dabbing her eyes, drying her fake tears. From behind the tissue though, she shot me a look that could have turned me to stone! I knew what she was thinking: don't you dare say a word! That was the message, loud and clear! And how could I? Who'd believe me?

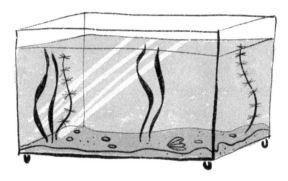

A week later, the Class Three goldfish vanished from their tank. There was a school inquisition, but nobody owned up. In the end, Mrs Poplar decided that a sea-gull must have got in when the windows were open and no-one was around. (A James Bond seagull, I thought. It would have had to be – stealth, timing, speed! And it took the lid off the tank and put it back on afterwards!)

FUR ELISE

I knew it was Elise, but I couldn't prove it, so there was no point saying anything. Every time it was mentioned, she went all wide-eyed and started on about how frightened the poor little things must have been. She ought to know, I thought. But I kept quiet.

I thought maybe it was over after that. I hoped so. But then, the day before yesterday, our cat disappeared. I know cats do that sometimes, but not Jamal. He's getting on a bit, and he hardly goes out at all. He hasn't missed his dinner a single time in the last couple of years!

Mum's been outside the last two nights, calling for him, and my brother's posted about it online. My sister's printed 'Missing' notices to put up all round the area. The trouble is, I'm pretty sure there's no point. I reckon it's too late to save Jamal.

The reason I say that is because the first evening he didn't come home, an ambulance turned up opposite. A few minutes later, it whizzed off with sirens going and lights flashing. We didn't see who they'd picked up, but Elise was off school yesterday. Miss March didn't say anything about it, but there are rumours that Elise is in a coma in hospital, after she blacked out. People have heard she choked on something, but nobody seems to know what. I bet I do. And I bet it was black and white.

FUR ELISE

So I'm really sad to say that it's probably RIP Jamal. I'll never know for sure, I guess, unless he suddenly turns up. I'd be astonished, though. Surely it's all over for him! Not a good way to go, poor old cat!

All the same, if he takes Elise down with him, it won't have been in vain. I've got my fingers crossed. Hopefully, Jamal's death is going to make the world a better place!

The Sting

I remember the day Hassan started at our school. I'm sure he remembers it too. It must have been so stressful for him!

I mean, imagine it the other way round. Imagine walking into your new school in Syria! The buildings are different, the classrooms, the clothes, the food, the work is all different, everyone looks totally different. And of course, they all speak a different language to you, so you can't read the books or the signs on the walls, and everyone is just babbling around you.

A lot of the girls crowded round Hassan that first morning, and I guess he probably realised they were trying to be friendly, but they were asking him a zillion questions, and I could see he had no idea what they were saying.

I stayed back then, even though I was really curious about him. I always am when people aren't the same as me,

22

and I mean really not the same, like different culture, different language. I love how different we can be on the outside, especially when inside we all want the same basic things – shelter, food, love, friends.

No, I stayed back because I was afraid he'd be feeling totally overwhelmed. I wondered, too, if he might not be comfortable talking to girls, because I didn't know if he'd gone to school with girls back in Syria. I know now, and the answer is yes, and he's fine with us, including girls like me with blue eyes and fair hair. I don't look anything like Hassan's sisters or any of the other girls he grew up with.

Hassan himself is olive-skinned, with dark eyes and black, black hair. The first time I set eyes on him, I thought he was beautiful, and a bit mysterious, too. I assumed everyone else would be as fascinated by him as I was. It didn't cross my mind there would be anyone in the class who didn't want him there. I guess Hassan picked up on that way before I did.

It took a while for him to start to settle in, of course. To begin with, he had an interpreter who came to see him at school a couple of times a week, and they'd go out of class together with the T.A. or sometimes our teacher, Mr McFarren. I'd have loved to go with them. I taught myself a bit of Arabic at home, because I thought it might be nice for

Hassan to feel somebody was interested in where he came from.

There was someone else who was interested as well: Jack. He was definitely interested in where Hassan came from, but not in a good way. It was him I heard first using the word 'refugee' about Hassan, which of course he is. His family fled from the war in Syria and came to England in search of a new life. It's something people have done for millennia, I suppose, moved away from trouble to start again somewhere safe. So it wasn't what Jack said, so much as the way he said it.

He was quite subtle with the bullying at the beginning. I had no idea there was anything going on at all, and I'm sure Mr McFarren didn't know either. When Hassan and I became friends, I found out that Jack had started his campaign on day one. Hassan says he recognised the look in Jack's eyes, and the tone of the muttering, though he couldn't understand what Jack was saying. He didn't really care, he says. It was nothing to what he'd come from, the bombs and the shooting, and the constant fear. What was a bit of classroom bullying compared to a war zone?

I know what Hassan means, but I don't see it like that. There used to be this girl called Mallory who was really mean to me. I remember crying every day for a month in Year Two because I didn't want to go to school. I was *so* glad she left in Year Three.

Once I realised what Jack was up to – way after Hassan noticed – I wondered if I ought to do something about it. I didn't say anything though, because to start off with it was small stuff – Jack giving Hassan evils across the classroom, and whispering and passing notes. I don't know how he managed not to get caught, but Mr McFarren didn't pick up on it.

Once Hassan started to find his feet in the playground, Jack moved the battle out there too. Hassan was a very good footballer, it turned out, which Jack didn't like. Jack brought his own football to school every day. He decided who was going to play with it and he wasn't going to let Hassan join in, that was for sure! When Hassan asked, Jack refused. Hassan went off and sat on the bench under the chestnut tree. The next day, Hassan asked someone else – Toby, I think – but because it was Jack's ball, Toby didn't dare say yes.

The third day, before Hassan could be turned down, I went and got a football from the P.E. store and made gestures to him to kick it around with me. Sophie, who's in the year above, came over straight away to play with us. She's a very good player, but I hadn't known because Jack's never let her play either because she's a girl. Me, Hassan and Sophie had fun, even though I'm a bit rubbish and there were only the three of us. Sophie and Hassan took it in turns to do some really cool skills while I just watched in awe!

That was the first time I saw Hassan smile, and also the first time I realised how much Jack hated him. Quite a few of the boys who were playing with Jack were eyeing Hassan, obviously wondering if they could come and join us. The following day, one of them, Sam, braved it and brought his own ball to school. A couple of others left Jack's game, too, and came to play with us. By the end of the day, though, Sam's ball was flat – it had somehow got a tear in it – so that was the end of that.

For a while, Jack carried on trying to make Hassan's life miserable in as many little ways as he could think of, stopping him sitting down at the lunch table, yanking Hassan's stuff off the pegs in the cloakroom so his coat got kicked round the floor, barging into him in the corridor.

Once, I heard him hiss something about refugee scroungers, and another time it was something about Hassan's dad taking someone else's job. I don't know if Hassan's English was good enough by then to understand exactly what Jack was saying, but he'd got the point already: as far as Jack was concerned, Hassan wasn't welcome.

Jack's campaign had been quietly building, day on day, and I'm ashamed to say I still hadn't done anything about it. And then there was the incident with the shoes. We'd just had P.E., and had come back in to get changed. Jack was stuffing his P.E. clothes back in his kit when he saw Hassan pick up one of his shoes by the toe and tap the heel of it on the floor before he put it on.

"What's the saddo doing?" Jack asked Noah next to him, not very quietly. Noah is one of Jack's sidekicks, always hanging around nearby, ready to say, 'Yeah, Jack. No, Jack. Great plan, Jack!' There's another sidekick, too, Ethan, who's dumber than Noah but otherwise the same. I think of them as Crabbe and Goyle to Jack's Malfoy, though Jack isn't as handsome as Malfoy.

Anyway, Noah and Ethan both looked at Hassan, who had just picked up the second shoe and was about to do the same thing. They smirked idiotically.

"What you doing?" Noah asked Hassan.

Hassan looked up and replied in a stream of Arabic.

"No understandy!" mocked Jack. "Speak English!"

Hassan frowned. "Look for ..." he began hesitantly. Then he said another word or phrase in Arabic. He put the shoe down and used both hands to form an odd shape, making a pinching motion with the thumb and first finger of his right hand, and holding the first finger of his left hand about ten centimetres behind it, curled over at the top.

"Dunno what you're talking about!" Jack sneered. He turned to his mates. "I reckon the freak was looking for something in his shoes! Maybe he thinks someone left him a present!"

Noah and Ethan sniggered obligingly.

"What's all this, boys?" asked Mr McFarren coming into the room.

"Nothing, Sir," Jack said innocently. "I was just interested to know why Hassan was knocking his shoes on the floor."

Mr McFarren smiled at Hassan. "Habit, I expect," he said. "If you spend any time living in a place where there are scorpions, you always knock out your shoes before you put them on. Was that it, Hassan? Scorpion?" He made a shape with his hands very like the shape Hassan had made.

Hassan nodded enthusiastically. "Scor-pion?" he repeated.

"That's right. But we don't have scorpions in the UK, or at least there are some but they're very rare indeed." Seeing Hassan's face, the teacher said more simply, "No scorpions here."

Hassan nodded again and smiled.

That was the end of it for the time being, but the following week, when we came in from P.E. to get changed, Hassan must have remembered Mr McFarren's remark, because he didn't tap his shoes on the floor. Instead, he just started to put them on. When he got to the second shoe, though, he gave a shout, and kicked it across the room. I looked immediately at Jack. He and his sidekicks were sniggering again.

"What's all this, Hassan?" Mr McFarren asked, picking up the shoe. "You shouldn't throw your shoes, you know. You might hurt someone."

Hassan had gone pale and was staring at something on the floor behind the table leg. Then he looked at Jack who was grinning from ear to ear. He bent down and picked up a rubber scorpion and held it out on his palm. Its tail waved quite convincingly.

Mr McFarren frowned. "Whose is that?" he asked sharply.

Nobody answered. Jack and the other two had wiped their faces blank. Hassan narrowed his eyes and put the rubber scorpion in his pocket.

One of the T.A.s from another class came to the door then, and Mr McFarren had to go out, otherwise he probably wouldn't have dropped the subject so soon. When he came back later though, he was preoccupied and had forgotten all about it.

Rubber scorpions kept turning up all over the place after that. Jack must have ordered a whole load of them off the internet. Every time Hassan found one – in his drawer, in the hood of his coat, in his water bottle even – he kept it. He didn't say anything, just put it in his pocket and carried on with what he was doing. I think he was determined to take care of this on his own, without going to Mr McFarren. He did take care of it, too!

He'd have done it sooner, he told me afterwards, if only

he'd had the money. When he said that, I wished I'd made the effort to get to know him quicker – I'd have happily paid for what he wanted out of my pocket money. In June, though, it was Hassan's birthday, and his uncle sent him some money from Syria. It was the first money of his own he'd had since he'd arrived in England. It wasn't quite enough, he said, but he persuaded his sister to lend him the rest.

He sent off to the website and waited anxiously for the post every day for a week. When it arrived, he had to wait again until Thursday came round and we had P.E. again.

When I think back, I remember he was starting to come out of himself a bit more around that time. He smiled more often, and his English was getting better by the day.

But as Hassan got happier and more confident, Jack got angrier. I saw the dirty looks, and I saw him in a huddle at playtime with Noah and Ethan. In fact, on that Thursday I had decided to stay behind for a few minutes at the end of school and talk to Mr McFarren, before Jack did something really nasty.

In the afternoon, we had our P.E. lesson outside – tennis – and when we came in, Jack was already back in the classroom, having managed as usual to avoid helping put everything away. As I put my cardigan on, he was shoving his feet into his shoes.

Suddenly, he screamed. It was a full-throated scream of terror and pain, and it went on and on.

Everyone stopped what they were doing and stared. Still screaming, Jack hopped on the spot and dragged his shoe off. He hurled it across the room and clutched his socked foot in both hands. His scream became a high-pitched wail. Sweat broke out on his forehead. His skin went white and clammy.

"What's going on?" thundered Mr McFarren. "Stop that noise, Jack! Whatever you've done, it can't be that painful!"

Jack was gibbering now, unable to string two words together.

Across the table from me, I heard Hassan mutter, "No understandy! Speak English!" He sidled across the room to where Jack's shoe had landed and crouched down. When he straightened up, he had the shoe in one hand, and a drawing pin and one of Jack's rubber scorpions in the other. He held them out towards Mr McFarren.

"Caught with your own trick!" The teacher burst out laughing. "I saw one of those scorpions on the floor the other day. Bella said it was yours. And now Hassan has got his own back on you for taking the mickey out of him!" He gave a hoot. "Nice one, Hassan!"

Hassan grinned. He put the drawing pin on the desk, and slipped the rubber scorpion into his pocket alongside the matchbox containing the live scorpion.

Jack left our school soon after that. His parents were furious that their complaint to the headteacher wasn't taken seriously. It was racism, they claimed, the school not investigating what Jack said had happened.

The hospital confirmed that Jack seemed somehow to have been stung by a scorpion, and gave him the correct anti-venom. It wasn't a Syrian variety, which was probably just as well. Hassan told me later they're called Deathstalkers, because their venom is enough to kill a small child. Jack isn't small, but it would have been a lot worse than the sting he actually got. Apparently, this one was a relatively harmless Indonesian type, sometimes kept as a pet.

Except for the original shoe incident, there was nothing to link the scorpion sting to Hassan. He said he didn't know anything about a real, live scorpion, and he was wise enough to keep quiet about the rubber scorpions too.

THE STING

Mr McFarren stuck by him through all the questions from the headteacher, and various other people, which made me think our teacher may have had a better idea than I'd realised what Jack was up to.

Hassan had to rehome the scorpion of course, quickly, before his parents could hear about the accusation. I didn't fancy it, but my brother was super keen, so it now lives in a tank in his room. That was how Hassan and I came to be friends.

When he gave the scorpion to my brother, Hassan thought it needed a name. The three of us went through loads of possibilities, but we couldn't think of anything that really fitted, except for 'Jack', which would have been much too obvious.

Then I had a brainwave. I grabbed a book from my brother's shelf and waved it at Hassan. He beamed from ear to ear. "That is the answer!" he said.

"It's perfect!" I was so chuffed he got what I meant!

"You're saying we should call it Harry Potter?" my brother asked, confused.

"No, you idiot!" I laughed.

Hassan and I spoke at the same time. "We're going to call it Malfoy!" And we did.

Unlucky for Some

Some people think Friday the thirteenth is unlucky. Not me. Friday the thirteenth is my lucky day.

I was born on Friday the thirteenth of June, 2008. It was really lucky that I was born that day because it was the only Friday the thirteenth that year. The next year was a bumper year: there were three, and three again in 2012, but there won't be another year like that now until 2026. I know. I've got a calendar on my wall with them all marked up.

You might be wondering why I care. Maybe you think I'm some sort of date freak. It isn't that. It's all to do with luck. Bad luck.

You know how a lightning conductor gives the lightning a safe way to get to the ground? Like it collects it? Well, I'm a sort of bad luck conductor. I collect bad luck so that other people don't have it. Black cats crossing your path.

Walking under ladders. Lone magpies. Getting pooed on by a bird – though actually, that's supposed to be lucky, weirdly! Maybe that's why I haven't managed it yet. I've waited underneath pigeons sitting on wires quite a few times, but they don't poo half as often as you'd think. If it was bad luck to get pooed on, I bet it would have happened to me more than once!

The way I see it, it's a calling: I was born to do this, or at least, it became my destiny from the moment my parents named me, because they called me Mallory. I know, you wouldn't guess it, would you? I mean, it's a pretty normal sort of name, maybe a bit American-sounding. We're not American, but my mum and dad liked it and so do I, I guess. All the same, I was a bit shocked when I looked it up, because Mallory means 'unlucky'!

When I asked Mum about it, she looked surprised and then she grinned. "I suppose that goes along with you being born on Friday the thirteenth," she said. "Just as well all that stuff's rubbish!"

That's where she's wrong, though. It isn't rubbish. She's just one of those people who can't make the connections between the omens and the bad things that happen. Most people are like that these days. They can't help it. It's the way their brains are wired.

Mine isn't, though. My brain is wired differently, more like people back in the past. What I mean is, in the old days, people used to be much better at making connections, much more in tune with the world around them, without the distraction of smartphones and all that. Ever since the dawn of time, in fact, people have watched the skies; they've watched the animals and birds; and they've worked out how things fitted together. Back in the past, they understood that eclipses cause sickness and famine, and they noticed other signs too, that people wouldn't see today.

They always knew that 1666 was going to be an unlucky year, for example, because if you write out the year in Roman numerals, they line up in order of size: MDCLXVI. You see that? So, long before the baker's fire was lit – the one that turned into the Great Fire of London – they knew something bad was on the way. I think it's sad that we've lost that talent over time, or at least most people have. I'm glad I haven't.

I can hear you wondering if I'm serious about this. I totally am. You might even be thinking, What is she talking about? Don't worry if that's how you feel. You won't offend me. I'm used to it. It's a bit like how superheroes have to live under cover, with nobody knowing their powers or understanding what it's like to be them. My situation is a lot like that, in fact. Absorbing bad luck for other people really is my superpower, because I not only have the gift to recognise omens, I'm also not affected by the bad luck they bring.

I guess you'd like some proof. That's fair enough, but it's also a bit tricky. I'm sure you can understand that when I absorb the omens and stop something bad from happening, that thing doesn't happen. It's a bit like MI6 - or whoever - preventing a terrorist attack. There is no attack. MI6 has succeeded, which means that nothing happens. It can be quite hard to prove afterwards that something was going to happen before you stopped it.

Sometimes, the best way to show it is through something that should have been much worse, like the time my mum fell down the stairs the week after she hung the new mirror on the landing. Hanging the mirror wasn't the problem, it was the fact she started to drop it. Seven years bad luck you get if you smash a mirror! I came out of my room and realised what was about to happen and dived to catch it. I didn't quite manage – it was way too big and heavy for me to hold by one corner – but my efforts did mean that when the glass smashed, it wasn't Mum who did it. It was my hands the mirror passed through just before it hit the floor, so I got the full force of the bad luck from it. That was a good a thing because Mum fell down the stairs the following week. Fortunately, she only sprained her ankle instead of breaking it, or worse, breaking her neck!

She doesn't realise that was thanks to me. She has no idea how lucky it was that I was there! She was too busy being cross about the mirror. She hadn't been going to drop it, she reckoned, but she was distracted by me leaping across the landing. I didn't argue when she said that. I just smiled to myself and let it go. I learnt that lesson when Dad backed our car into old Mrs Fitch's wall, which is another example of things turning out better than they would have done without me.

Mrs Fitch is our next door neighbour, and she wasn't very happy about her wall. According to Dad, he was distracted by something on the radio, and the wall is too low to see in the rear-view mirror. What he didn't realise was that I'd shooed three separate lone magpies off the lawn during breakfast – one being for sorrow, as I'm sure you know. Because I'd done that, when Dad was reversing towards the wall, Mrs Fitch's cat jumped down out of the way, and not on the side of the wall where it would have got squashed either. If I'd let those magpies hang about, that cat would be dead!

I tried to comfort Dad by telling him this, but he was annoyed at himself for knocking the wall down because it was going to cost us to get it fixed. He shouted at me like he's never done before. I forgave him, of course, though not right away, I have to admit. Once I'd forgiven him, I made a mental note to myself not to bother trying to explain these things to people in the future. They just don't get it.

That was my resolution until this week, and I'd stuck to it, too. But on Tuesday, I found someone who seems to understand.

It came about when I was looking on the internet. I've been hunting for omens I hadn't come across before, in case there were other ways of absorbing bad luck that I hadn't already thought of. And you'll never guess what I found? An internet chat room about all kinds of threats to the country!

It's amazing, this site. There's all sorts on there that the government doesn't have the faintest idea about! You'd never even think of some of them! Conspiracies to kidnap the Queen and Prince Charles and Prince William, so we don't have a Head of State! Rogue scientists creating deadly viruses that could wipe out the whole of the UK! Computer geeks plotting to hack into loads of different systems at once!

That's a great one, actually. You know people have these smart toasters and kettles that are internet-enabled, sitting on their kitchen sides? Well, there are guys out there planning to hack into all of them at the same moment. They're going to swamp the electricity network with a sudden demand for power by switching them all on together, and they're going to bring down the internet with them at the same time! The whole country is going to go down, and who knows how long it'll take for everything to get back up and running again? Meanwhile, they'll be able to cause all kinds of havoc!

As you can imagine, I was pretty excited when I found this, and a bit worried too, if I'm honest. I mean, this was big stuff I'd stumbled across, and I couldn't think what to do to stop it happening. The only thing I knew for sure was that it had to be someone like me who did, and I didn't know anyone else like me.

41

Then, I had a real stroke of luck – I do get good luck as well as bad luck – because I saw someone in the chat threads called Chelsea who lives in Bermondsey, and who's really into this sort of thing like me. I messaged her directly, and we've got loads in common! We both have the gift to see connections that other people can't see, we both collect omens, and we're both thirteen years old. I'm guessing her gift isn't as strong as mine because her name doesn't mean much, and she wasn't born on Friday the thirteenth, but even so, it was great to find her.

And get this! Tomorrow, we have the most incredible chance to absorb enough bad luck in one go to cancel out every single thing mentioned on that website! How amazing is that?

I bet you're wondering what it is that's powerful enough to do that. Well, the first part, you should be able to guess, because today is Thursday the twelfth of August, which means? Exactly. Tomorrow is Friday the thirteenth, which is the perfect day to take action.

And the other part? There are thunderstorms forecast all over London tomorrow afternoon. If we're really lucky, they'll come in early, in time for one o'clock, which is 13:00 hours, of course. That would be a pretty long shot, getting a lightning strike at exactly the right time.

Even without that though, we have a plan, me and Chelsea. We're going to watch the radar to see where the storms are, and then we're going to meet at the top of Parliament Hill, which is a really high point near where I live. We'll need some sort of metal rod, we realised, to draw the lightning down, and we can't carry anything too big on the tube. But I've solved that problem already.

In case you're wondering, we're not in any danger – you don't necessarily get killed by a lightning strike, even when you're an ordinary person. Mary Anning was struck by lightning and it didn't kill her. Besides, Chelsea and I both know already that we're not affected by the bad luck we collect. And just think of the power! Two thirteen year old girls, one called Mallory and born on Friday the thirteenth, struck by lightning on Friday the thirteenth! There's no better way to collect bad luck than that, is there?

The Times
Saturday 14 August

The bodies of two thirteen year old girls were discovered this morning at the top of Parliament Hill, apparently struck by lightning. A home-made metal structure was found on the ground next to the bodies, built from wire coat-hangers. Investigators speculate that the girls had made a lightning conductor, unaware of the danger to themselves.

It isn't yet known whether these tragic deaths are connected to a cyber attack, launched on Friday afternoon, which immobilised the electricity network and paralysed internet and mobile communications. Rail and underground networks ground to a halt, and businesses and homes were left in darkness after hackers successfully took over thousands of internet-enabled domestic appliances.

During the power outage, a man was also intercepted in the grounds of Buckingham Palace, apparently intending to kidnap the Queen. Investigations into possible links between the deaths and the cyber attacks are ongoing.

Piggy in the Middle

I love school trips. I don't much care where we go. Getting out of school is enough! As far as I'm concerned, it's great just going off on a coach, flicking paper pellets at the kids in front, scoffing bits of your school packed lunch, and singing at the top of your voice!

Even better if it's all outdoors when you get there, as long as it's not throwing it down with rain. I'm not great in the classroom, I have to admit. I'm definitely going to have a job that lets me be outside when I'm older: anything, as long as I'm not stuck at a desk staring at a screen.

Things feel so different when you're not in school together – it isn't just that you're in your own clothes somewhere else. It's more than that. People behave a bit differently. Sometimes it's great fun. Sometimes it's a disaster. Whatever else it is, it definitely isn't boring!

You won't be surprised to know that I was really looking

forward to our trip to Durrington Home Farm. I guess some of you might be thinking a school trip to a farm isn't the most exciting thing ever. Who knows, some of you might even be lucky enough to live on a farm. I don't. I live on the seventh floor of a tower block, so I was pretty happy to get out of London for a day, to a real farm too, not one of these city farms that's more like a second-rate zoo with pigs and sheep instead of lions.

I wasn't the only one who was excited about this trip to the farm, actually. Most of us were, even the ones who were pretending they weren't. I mean, you don't get many animals around Bermondsey; only people's pets and the odd rat! So this was a proper change. It wasn't raining either, which was the first time it had let up for about two weeks. Our teacher, Miss Ullah, looked at us in our trainers and jeans as we got on the bus, and sighed. She was in wellies, and the letter home had said wellies, because of the mud. The trouble is, at least half of us – including me – don't have them, and the rest wouldn't be seen dead in them.

Lily reckoned she was one of the 'wouldn't be seen dead in them' kids, though I'd bet she didn't own a pair of wellies either. She said she did, but she was in leggings with sparkly bits and a pair of super tall, white trainers. She hadn't brought a coat either, most likely because it wasn't

46

cool. I heard Miss Ullah asking just before registration if the office should ring her mum to drop one in before we left, but Lily said no. Miss Ullah pointed out that it might rain. Lily said she didn't care.

That's Lily all over. She doesn't care about anything. She wears her hair in a ponytail right on top of her head and turns her school skirt over at the waist to make it shorter. She complains about not being allowed to wear make-up to school, even though this is junior school, and when I saw her in the street one Saturday with some other girls, they honestly looked like they were about fifteen, not ten or eleven, in their high heels and tight T-shirts.

My mum has always tutted when she's seen Lily, and says she'll be pushing a pram along the street by the time she is fifteen. At the moment though, I'm supposed to be nice to Lily because she was friends with that girl, Chelsea Thingummy, from Manor Grove Academy – the one who got killed by lightning. I get what Mum means, but there's no point being nice to Lily. If I even talk to her, I just get a mouthful back. So I've gone on ignoring her which suits me fine. She's incredibly annoying, especially the way she's so set on not being interested in anything.

Anyway, Lily was sitting near the back of the coach next to Ella-Mae, both of them chewing gum and staring at

47

Lily's phone, which she wasn't supposed to have with her. When Miss Ullah came up the coach, Lily slipped the phone away and she and Ella-Mae both stopped chewing, like two cows who've been freeze-framed. Me and Rory were kneeling up on our seats, talking to Elijah and Zac in the seats behind, and I saw Lily roll her eyes. Miss Ullah had just said something about everyone being a bit noisy and over-excited. Ella-Mae rolled her eyes too, trying to be as cool as Lily. It was so pathetic! As soon as Miss Ullah had gone back down to the front, the phone came out and the chewing started up again.

Lily was in my group for the day, worst luck, though at least Miss Ullah had split her up from Ella-Mae. That was the idea, anyway. We were in groups of six, each with a parent, so me, Rory and Harrison were with Lily and two other girls called Niamh and Scarlett. I'm Olly, by the way, in case you were wondering.

We had Harrison's mum as our adult. Harrison didn't seem to mind, which I thought was a bit weird. I mean, I wouldn't particularly want my mum to come on a school trip, and she's way too busy at work to take time off for these things anyway. But if she did come, I wouldn't want to be in her group.

Harrison's a bit wet, though, and when I met his

mum, I could see why. She was such a drip! "Be careful of this! Mind that! Don't do such and such!" I can see that might sound like she was telling us off all the time, but it was more like a panicky squeak every other minute. I tried to say that we've seen nettles before – just because we're city kids, doesn't mean we don't know what they are. I've been stung climbing over railings, or poking around on bits of wasteland. Then I realised Harrison probably isn't allowed out to do that sort of thing.

I was saying about Lily and Ella-Mae being separated, which they were supposed to be. The problem was, as each group started off round the farm on a kind of circuit, Ella-Mae's group was behind ours. So Lily just dawdled and hung back to gossip with her. We kept on and on having to wait while Harrison's mum scurried back to get her. I don't know why she bothered. I thought we should have left Lily and Ella-Mae on the coach, for all the interest either of them were showing in anything. The man from the farm who was taking us round obviously thought the same. I saw him shake his head a couple of times.

Like I said earlier, the farm was a proper one, maybe a bit old-fashioned I suppose, with lots of different kinds of animals, and not many of each, rather than a million cows standing around in barns. There *were* cows, but they were in a field with a really grumpy-looking bull and a totally unnecessary *Beware of the Bull* sign. As though anyone in their right mind would go near him!

The farm was really well set up for school kids, because there were loads of things you could actually do. Rory and I both had a go at milking a goat, which is a lot harder than you'd think, and they had some fleeces you could shear to see what it might be like trying to shear a sheep. That wasn't easy either, when you consider that the fleece was lying flat and still, whereas the sheep would be thrashing around.

They let us try to catch one of the sheep too, like we'd have to if we were going to shear it. I wondered if that was a bit mean to the sheep until I saw how easily it scampered off. It stood at the other end of the pen and bleated at us just like it was laughing. Even with three of us, we couldn't corner it and keep hold of it.

Anyway, the day passed pretty quickly. We ate lunch on some benches in the sunshine, and there was a wooden adventure playground we were allowed on. I thought Harrison's mum was going to have kittens, she was so frantic about Harrison. By the end of the day, I was feeling quite sorry for him.

Lily, on the other hand, was getting on everyone's nerves, moaning about how bored she was, and when were we going home? She spent half the lunch hour in the loos, fiddling with her hair, and putting on make-up, which Miss Ullah made her clean off as soon as she came out. Honestly, what's wrong with her? She'd been tiptoeing round the farm all day in her stupid shoes, and she hadn't stopped whingeing about the mud! I found myself almost wishing it would rain, so she'd get wet without her coat.

Something happened that was much better than that though, something that made this probably the best school trip I will ever go on!

It was the end of the afternoon, and the whole class was listening to a talk about pigs from the man who'd been with our group all day. There were three different kinds, he said: the Berkshires, which were black; the Tamworths which had gingery fur; and the Gloucester Old Spots, which were (you guessed it!) spotty. They were all pretty good-natured he said, except if they had piglets, which one of the Tamworths did. The sows could get quite grumpy if they thought their piglets might be in danger. The Tamworth had thirteen, which was an unusually large litter.

He told us a few things about pigs, like how they're not dirty like everyone thinks – they always poo in one place, he said, not everywhere, and they have to wallow in the mud to cool down because they can't sweat. The mud protects their skin from the sun, too, so they don't get sun burnt.

After that, he asked for a volunteer to help feed them. I don't think he actually wanted a real volunteer, though, because quite a few of us put our hands up and he didn't choose any of us. Instead, he picked Lily. She was standing behind me, and when I turned round, no way had she had her hand up. You should have seen her face!

"Me?!" she said, between chews.

"Yes, you." The man from the farm had this big, wide grin.

Lily shuffled forward. I don't know if she even knew what she was helping with – I bet she hadn't been listening!

The man got her to climb over into the pig pen, and she did it, but she stood there like she'd been pinned to the fence, trying not to step in the ankle deep mud!

Then he passed her a muddy bucket of something sloppy and greyish.

You should have heard how she wailed! "This is well heavy!" I guess it was, but it was the way she was holding it too, trying not to let it touch her top and leggings. "It's disgusting! What is it?"

"Cooked porridge, fish meal and milk powder," the man said. "You prefer this one?"

Lily peered into his bucket, then sort of lurched away, her face all twisted up. The rest of us leaned forward. The other bucket was full of mouldy fruit and vegetables, peelings, and bits of something brown. It smelled pretty rank, like the bins sometimes do.

The man laughed. "I'm not sure it's any lighter, actually," he said. "Anyway, I thought you'd sooner feed the piglets. My bucket is for this lot over here," and he jerked his head to a gang of young pigs pushing each other about in the next pen. "I want you to take yours to the piglet trough." He pointed.

"I don't see any piglets!" Lily said, quite stroppy.

"Don't you worry! They'll come running as soon as

53

they hear you!" The man chuckled. "Just tip it in, and get out of the way."

So Lily minced off round the edge of the pig pen, trying to keep clear of the mud and not spill the feed down herself. It was obvious she was in a right old hump. Most of us had started giggling. I mean, I'd have loved to feed the piglets, but this was funnier. Miss Ullah tried to shush us, and called to Lily that she was doing really well, but I could see she wanted to laugh.

Sure enough, exactly like the farmer said, the second Lily tipped the feed into the trough, the piglets came shooting out of the sty like thirteen little brown rockets. Lily's eyes went really wide. I guess the piglets weren't that small and she thought they were running at her! Did she do what she'd been told, though? Course not! She hadn't listened, so she didn't move.

As the piglets got to her, she dropped the bucket. Two piglets threw themselves into it, then realised it was empty, and shot out again. Lily tried to jump out of the way, but by now she was in totally the wrong place! Thirteen gingery little bodies were pushing and biting round her ankles and treading on her precious shoes to get at the food in the trough before their brothers and sisters.

Lily started making this high-pitched mewing sound,

totally panicked! For a few seconds, it looked like she was frozen, then she tried to step out of the crush of noshing piglets. She must have trodden on one, because it squealed furiously and whipped round, as though it wanted to bite her.

Lily shrieked and leapt in the air! It didn't take much for her to slip in the mud as she landed. She went down, flailing her snowy trainers – which were more or less black by this time – and accidentally kicked another two piglets as she fell. There was more furious squealing, only this time, we could hear a deeper grunting noise, too. At the opening of the sty stood the sow who must have heard the noise her babies had made.

Lily was now lying on her back in the mud and one of the smallest piglets decided to climb onto her chest, to get to the food better. At the same time, the mother pig lumbered forward. Lily saw it and screamed.

It's hard to say whether the pig was properly wound up, though it was dead easy to see Lily wasn't helping things. Whatever, the farmer decided not to chance it. He jumped over the fence from the next door pen and grabbed a long pole. "Get up!" he shouted at Lily.

"I'm stuck!" Lily howled. "I can't move! Get this evil little beast off of me!"

The farmer was holding the stick like a lance, using it to keep the sow at bay. "Just stand up!" he yelled.

"My trainers! My leggings! I'm filthy! Ow!" Lily was trying to sit up and turf the piglet off her, but it was hanging in there, scrabbling about on her lap with its sharp little trotters, trying to get back to the trough.

"Get up, NOW!" shouted the farmer. The sow was pushing against the stick which wasn't very thick. She looked quite bad-tempered, even though the piglets had got back to feeding.

Lily scrambled to her feet, slipping and sliding all over the place.

"Over the fence! Out!" the man yelled.

56

Lily clambered up the wooden rail and sort of slumped over it onto our side. Her hands and clothes were black and sticky. Her trainers were invisible inside giant clods of mud, and her hair was full of the stuff, too. Where she'd caked herself in make-up at lunchtime, her face was now smeared with oily black streaks. She looked like a monster out of a swamp as she staggered towards us. We couldn't hold back any longer. We just burst out laughing! So did Miss Ullah.

The farmer backed away from the sow, then dropped the stick and swung himself over the fence into the other pig pen. The mother Tamworth broke into a run and charged, not at him but at us. She crashed into the fence where Lily had just climbed over, grunting angrily. Thank God, the fence held!

Lily burst into tears. Ella-Mae stepped away, then remembered she was supposed to be Lily's friend. She inched back towards her, looking embarrassed. "Come on, girl," she muttered. "It's only a bit of mud." But Lily wasn't having any of it. Here was the chance to throw a hysterical fit, and she was absolutely going to throw one!

While she did that, and the rest of us watched and sniggered, Miss Ullah talked to the farmer. He looked a bit sheepish, but I could see Miss Ullah wasn't really cross with him. In fact, I got the feeling he'd done something she'd have loved to do, but would never be allowed.

On the coach home, Lily sat on her own looking like thunder. Miss Ullah had made her change into the random bits of school uniform she'd brought from lost property just in case something like this happened. She'd helped Lily rinse the worst of the mud out of her hair in the loos, but the coach driver had still insisted on covering Lily's seat in bin bags to keep it clean.

The rest of us, including Ella-Mae, were crowded together towards the front of the bus because there was a definite smell hanging around Lily. Maybe she'd stumbled through the bit of the pen where the pigs pooed. Whatever it was, it was vile!

I'd love to say that after this amazing school trip, Lily was a changed person and started listening in class and not endlessly faffing over what she looked like. Unfortunately, that would be a total lie. She did keep coming to school, which was something, I suppose – I honestly thought she might start bunking off. If anything, though, she was worse than before.

When I was grumbling to Mum about that the other day, she just laughed.

"Of course Lily is still Lily," she said. "A bit of mud

was never going to change that. At least the rest of you got a really good laugh!" She thought for a sec and then she grinned. "You know what they say?"

"What?"

"You can put lipstick on a pig, but it's still a pig!"

A Load of Bull

I reckon in every class of every school in the country there's at least one kid who tells tall tales. I've never been in a class without one, and we're an army family so we've moved around quite a bit.

I even tried being one of those kids myself, just to see what it was like. It's one of the good things about changing schools so often – you can keep reinventing yourself, so you can try being different people. It's kind of interesting, although of course what you actually end up doing is trying to be the sort of kid that other kids can get on with quite easily. There's no point in making close friends though because you'll have to move on again soon enough, leaving your new BFF behind. I had one once, a BFF – Brody, he was called. After we moved, I didn't see him again. So much for forever!

It was quite fun for a while, being one of the tall tales

kids, thinking up new outrageous things to say. I can't remember all the things I came out with, but I did have a few favourites. One was that my parents were once at a really posh meal overseas, and they got served live cockerel to eat. Another one was that Tom Cruise came to my house for tea. And there was also one about a real dinosaur egg we used to have, with a fossilised baby dinosaur in it.

I realised pretty quickly that you have to come up with things that can't be proved right or wrong: it's no good saying your mum used to be an Olympic athlete, or someone will want to know her name and look her up. My all-time best was the one about my dad picking me up from school by helicopter in his last job. A lot of kids wanted to see a photo of that, but I just said – super cool – that we never thought of taking pictures because it happened every day, so it was no big deal. (I had to think up a different excuse for having no photos of me with Tom Cruise – I said he had to be really careful about publicity, so he asked us not to take any. Oh, and the dinosaur egg had sadly got broken in one of our moves.)

After a bit, I have to say it did get tiring. I started to run out of ideas, and when I got to the next school, I dropped it. There was another reason I dropped it as well, which was that actually I find the kids who tell tall tales really annoying. I mean, they must know they're doing it! They haven't really had an eagle land on their bird table, or been picked out of the crowd at the circus to ride a motorbike through a ring of flame. Neither of those things is impossible, I suppose, but they're incredibly unlikely, especially when you consider that these particular stories were told to me by the same kid. It irritates me that the child telling these lies – let's face it, 'tall tales' is just a nice way of saying 'lies' – thinks I'm stupid enough to believe them! How can they not see that they're the ones who look stupid for being such rubbish liars?

Anyway, it took me less than half a day at my latest school to figure out which of the kids in my new class was The One. I reckon that any new kid to a class is a kind of magnet for the class fibber because they're the only person who hasn't already heard their incredible stories (and I literally mean 'incredible').

It was a boy this time round. I suppose the fact that

I'm also a boy might have drawn him out quicker too – I'm probably a better boasting target for another boy than if I were a girl. So this boy, George, started right away, out on the playground at morning break. "Hey, Nathan!" he called. Nathan is me, obviously. "You'll never guess what happened to me the other day!"

I wasn't even standing near him, which shows just how desperate he was for a new audience!

"What?" I said, instead of what I was actually thinking, which was, "Don't tell me – something totally unbelievable you just made up?" I was in polite mode, you see. It was the first morning of the first day, which I always think is a bit early to start making enemies. All the same, I clocked him there and then, before I even heard what he said next.

George put his shoulders back and puffed out his chest. I'm just wondering now: is it always the weedy kids who tell these kinds of stories? Now I think about it, I'm not sure I've ever known a big kid do it. I might check out that theory when I change schools again.

George said, "I was on my way home from school, and there was a bull that had got out of the field. It charged me, but I grabbed it by its horns and swung myself onto its back. It tried to throw me off, but I wouldn't let go."

"Wow!" I said. "That sounds amazing! Did you ride it home?"

George looked momentarily confused. Maybe he was taken aback that I hadn't rubbished him straight away.

"Er, no," he said. Then he had a burst of inspiration. "I wrestled it back into the field where it belonged and got it shut up properly."

I should say, by the way, that it wasn't completely impossible that there should have been a bull in a field between his house and school. The army base where my family is living at the moment is quite rural, so there's a fair bit of farmland around here.

"That's fantastic!" I said. I guess I sounded really enthusiastic. When I think back, I don't actually know why I was like that about it. Perhaps I was just in the mood to be nice. It can be dangerous though, with these kids: if you seem too interested – and too gullible – the class liar latches on to you and you end up hearing crazy stories practically every day.

That was what happened with George from then on. He decided I was his best friend and started following me around, endlessly trying to think of new things to impress me all the time.

I knew how to put a stop to it, of course. Needless to

say, I didn't believe a word of it: not about the teenager who pulled a knife on him outside the corner shop (it's not that kind of village, and the teenager didn't seem to want anything, which is what really let that story down); nor about his aunt and uncle winning the national lottery and wanting to stay anonymous (he was way too cool about that one. If it was true, he'd have been hopping with excitement about the expensive present they'd surely have bought him).

Like I say, I could have stopped it any time. All I had to do was diss him outright in front of the other kids. I didn't though, partly because that would have been super mean – which I'm not – and partly because I knew I wouldn't be at this school forever. Sooner or later, I'd move on and leave George behind. In the meantime, I thought it would be interesting to let it run on and see where it might lead.

Where it lead was not where I was expecting, though! No way!

George kept on about me going round to his house after school. I wasn't very keen, so I made every excuse I could think of – you know, swimming lessons, tutoring, judo, violin, whatever. It wasn't true, any of it: that kind of thing can be pretty hard to keep up when you're always moving round the country. That's why military kids often end up going to boarding schools, so they can do all that stuff and not have to keep starting over. George believed me, though. I guess it was way less weird than the stories he was making up himself!

I was doing fine with fending him off until the day of the school Christmas Fair. George got me to introduce our mums to each other, and straight away, George's mum told my mum how much they'd like to have me round after school. She said she knew how busy I was with all the things I did in the evenings, but was there a day in the week that

would work?

Mum looked a bit surprised, but said, yes, sure, that would be great. She was glad I'd made such a good friend.

I guess I should be grateful she didn't blow my cover and tell George's mum that I wasn't busy any evening, but I was more disappointed that she didn't take my hint. Sometimes grown-ups are so dense! I mean, why did she think I'd told George all that if not to avoid going to his house? Anyway, they arranged it for the next Friday, and there was no getting out of it.

So the following week, George and I were walking home from school together, back to his house. It was cold and bright, that nice winter weather you sometimes get, and I realised we were walking past a field of cows. I'd never been this way before, so I hadn't known they were there.

"Is this the field with the bull?" I asked George.

George kept on walking. I had the feeling he was weighing up his options. Before he'd answered, we reached a gate with a sign next to it. "Oh yeah, I guess it must be." I pointed. In actual fact, the 'Beware of the Bull' sign was faded and a bit wonky, so I figured there was a good chance there wasn't a bull in the field any more. Still, this was bound to be where the story had started, in George's head, and I sort of wanted him to know I'd sussed him.

A LOAD OF BULL

Then I saw the bull. It was out in the middle of the field, rubbing its flank against an oak tree. The cows, I noticed, were huddled together as far away as possible.

"You wrestled that?" I stopped. I was honestly a bit surprised that he'd dared make up a story about a beast like that! "He's massive!" I climbed the gate to get a better look. The bull was absolutely immense! It had huge shoulders, a big, thick ring through its nose, and a humongous pair of horns.

I looked round at George just in time to see the reluctance in his eyes.

"You must have been very high off the ground, up there on his back." Maybe that was a bit mean, but I couldn't resist it.

George obviously came to a decision. He bent down and picked up a large stone from the bottom of the hedge.

"That's right!" he said, with a pretty good effort at pride. "I showed him who's boss!" He climbed up onto the gate next to me and hurled the stone at the bull.

It was a very good throw, I'll say that. The bull was probably about fifteen metres away, but the stone struck it hard on one of its horns and bounced off, grazing its back. All the same, my opinion of George took a real nose-dive in that moment. I mean, who throws a stone at an animal for no reason? Seriously!

The bull clearly thought the same. It tossed its head and swung round. Seeing us, it left off rubbing itself against the tree and lumbered towards the gate. I jumped down and took a few steps back. The five-bar gate looked strong, but I didn't fancy pushing my luck.

George, however, saw his chance – as he thought – to impress me. He'd jumped down too, but was grabbing another stone. I winced. This time, the stone hit the bull straight between the eyes.

If we'd been in a cartoon, the bull would have swayed a bit and then fallen flat on its face. This wasn't a cartoon, though. The bull paused for a moment and shook its head as though trying to get rid of an annoying fly, then it glared at George and broke into a gallop towards him.

I was on the other side of the road by now, trying to become part of the opposite hedge, praying the gate would hold since there was no traffic around to come between me and this hulking piece of angry beef. George stood a couple of metres back from the gate, apparently more confident than I was that the bull couldn't get out. It was either brave or stupid. I knew which one I thought.

The next second, the full weight of the animal slammed into the gate.

The bars flexed. The catch rattled. The gate posts shuddered.

Fortunately, nothing gave.

"There you are!" George turned to me. He was pale. "He won't mess with us again." He turned and sauntered off down the road, humming to himself in a way that was totally put on.

"Won't mess with us?" I muttered, letting my breath out in a whistle. "More like can't mess with us, no thanks to you, George!"

I watched the bull. It felt unwise to take my eyes off it. The animal was breathing heavily through giant nostrils, sending out plumes of mist in the cold afternoon air, like a dragon about to breathe fire. Then it began to paw the ground, dragging its hoof through the mud, forward to back, forward to back. As far as the bull was concerned, its business with George was not finished. I hurried after my classmate, hoping it might calm down if we were both out of sight.

If only!

A few moments later, there was a sort of stampeding sound. The ground shook, like when a tank lumbers across a field during practice. Then the bull burst out of a gap in the hedge and landed squarely in George's path.

A LOAD OF BULL

It swung round to face him. It was properly snorting now, pumping out blasts of hot, wet breath, and it had started pawing the ground again. The noise of its hoof against the road was just like someone sharpening a knife.

George stopped dead in front of me. I heard him whimper faintly. I froze. George's school bag slipped to the ground. I'd like to say he was deliberately shedding it, but I'm not sure he knew it had fallen.

The bull shook its horns in a kind of flourish, then lowered its head and charged!

George squealed like a piglet and tried to jump out of the way. The bull was having none of it! It tossed its horns and caught George's coat on the tip of one. George was flung up into the air, landing across the bull's solid neck, floppy as a rag doll.

I leapt back into the hedge again as the bull careered past me and thundered down the road with George bouncing around on its back, well and truly skewered by his coat.

It must have taken me quite a bit longer than I realised to extract myself from the hedge. I guess I probably wasn't thinking all that clearly – part of my mind was still reeling with the shock of George being pronged like that. I stood on the road in a daze, trying to think what to do. I had no idea where George lived, so I couldn't run on to his house and tell his mum; I could phone home, but it would take too long for my own mum to get here; and the bungalows along this road looked like sheltered housing for old people.

I picked up George's school bag. The bull had carted him off the way we'd come, and we'd passed a shop not far back. I could get help there. I set off along the road after my idiotic classmate.

Outside the shop, I stopped short.

George lay crumpled on the ground, one of his arms twisted at an ominous angle. His coat was in shreds, his face was luminous white, and there was a bump the size of a cricket ball on his forehead. There was no sign of the bull.

What there was, however, was an older boy in a hoody standing with one foot on George's chest. He had a flick knife in one hand. Bizarrely, in the other, he seemed to be waving the local newspaper from the stand. I glanced at the headline. "CHRISTMAS COMES EARLY FOR £2M JACKPOT COUPLE!" yelled the front page.

"Don't make out you don't know them!" the teenager snarled at George. "They've got the same surname as you and they live round here! They must be your family!"

George whimpered again.

"I've just rescued you from a rampaging bull!" the

older boy shouted. "You're about to get a load of money off your auntie or whoever. I want a reward for helping you, or else!"

When my dad got his next posting a few months later, and I started at yet another school, I was tempted to tell them that I'd once been with a kid who'd been charged by a marauding bull, then saved by a teenager with a knife in return for money from his aunt and uncle's huge lottery win!

I didn't though. I didn't want to be known as the kid who tells tall tales.

Not now, Brody

Mrs Wilson was really very nice. Brody's mum was determined that this was so, having met her once at the supermarket, and there was no persuading her otherwise. It annoyed Brody because all the kids knew that the only reason Mrs Wilson had started working as a midday supervisor at the school was that she loved to lord it over children.

Mrs Wilson was a demon in the lunch hall, brandishing her cleaning spray like an automatic weapon, wiping you off your table the moment the last spoonful of dessert reached your mouth. Brody had often wondered if someone would keel over one day from disinfectant poisoning. It was as though Mrs Wilson was on a mission to erase every last trace of forensic evidence of these verminous children from the school hall.

Outside, she patrolled the playground with the

grimness of an army major whose latest bunch of recruits was a terrible disappointment. Brody knew his class wasn't particularly bad. Nor were any of the other classes actually, though Mrs Wilson maintained the whole lot of them were disobedient and rude. If you fell over and grazed your knee, she would march you inside, and while you were pinned to the chair she'd give you a lecture about how the children in previous years had been so much less rough, so much politer. If you believed what she said then the year-group who'd just left had been actual angels. But Brody had a brother in that year, so he knew this wasn't true. When he asked his brother, his brother said Mrs Wilson had always told children the same thing. It was pathetic, Brody thought. Did she really think kids didn't talk to each other?

Brody had got stuck in the chair once – only once, mind you – and had been on the receiving end of this tirade while Mrs Wilson swabbed his leg with enough antiseptic to sanitise an entire hospital. He was sure she used as much as possible because she knew it hurt. And there was no gentle dabbing either. It was rub, rub, rub! None of the other midday supervisors were like that. Since then, Brody had always got up as quickly as he could, dusted himself off and run on, even when his eyes watered with the pain. You didn't want to get caught.

The trouble was, it was more or less impossible to avoid Mrs Wilson. She seemed to be everywhere, storming across the hall or playground like she'd just been waiting for an excuse. One thing Brody particularly hated about her was the way she would make up rules on the spot, always things you weren't allowed to do or games you weren't allowed to play. It was no use appealing to the other supervisors either, even though some of them were teaching assistants. They just did what adults always do and stuck together.

"You need to listen to what Mrs Wilson tells you," they would say. "If she doesn't want you do something, there's bound to be a good reason."

Nobody ever specified what this reason might be, and Brody was sure he'd once seen Miss Taylor raise an eyebrow at Mrs Halliard when she said it. He hoped one of the teachers might say something, even perhaps Mr Pewsey, if everyone else was too chicken. But the headteacher just wrung his hands and approached Mrs Wilson with a face like a dog that expects to be kicked. No, it was a part of Brody's life at St. Andrew's Primary that Mrs Wilson was a law unto herself.

The day that changed was a Wednesday in May. The willows were in full leaf, which was more significant than it might seem, and the air was still and hot. The Reception children finished their lunch first, and came out in their sun hats to play on the main part of the playground, followed soon after by the Year Ones. The younger children didn't generally play on the field at lunch play, so they were unaware of the presence of a very unusual visitor inside the school grounds.

In the staff-room, one of the teachers was flicking through the news on her phone, but it was the national news she was looking at and the story hadn't travelled that far yet. It would. It would be one of the biggest stories of the year and would earn the children of St. Andrew's half a day off school a fortnight later, as well as all the fabulous disruption and distraction caused by the presence of journalists. That went on for some time after the police, fire service, ambulance crews, and zoo staff had gone.

The first Brody knew of it was the shrieks of a gaggle of Year Three girls who had wandered up the field to sit in the shade of the willow tunnel, and who now scattered. The tunnel had been planted two years before and had grown into quite a thicket, and the school's groundsman had begun this morning pruning the long fronds that had sprouted across the inside, so that the children would be able to go along it again. He'd begun at the far end, before being called away unexpectedly, which meant that what lay inside was invisible from the playground.

Brody watched the girls cluster together again at a safe distance, heads bent, seemingly comparing notes. Then one girl, Rashida, detached herself from the group and tiptoed over to the willow tunnel again. Curious, Brody headed up the field to see what had caused the kerfuffle.

He was half way across the grass when Rashida leapt backwards. "It is!" she shrieked. "There's a tiger!"

Brody broke into a trot, towards the willow tunnel rather than away from it, undeterred by Rashida pelting down the field past him. He wondered if he was making a mistake, but the mere thought that a tiger might be in the school grounds was both so exciting and so fantastically unlikely that he wanted to know the truth as soon as possible.

As he got close, he slowed down and crept forward quietly, as if he really were stalking a tiger. From just a few paces away, it was impossible to see anything through the blade-like leaves that covered the tunnel. Brody didn't feel sure there was anything to see anyway. True, Rashida had seemed genuinely scared, but logic decreed that it was much more likely she was somehow mistaken. Perhaps it was a large toy animal, put there as a joke by the groundsman, or perhaps ... Brody couldn't think of any other explanation.

About half a metre away, he stopped and stared into the willows, listening intently for the slightest noise. His heart had started to pound, getting louder with every beat so that it felt like it might be enough to frighten the fiercest animal away. There was no chance of hearing a tiger's breathing over that, not that a soft toy would breathe.

Then, between the leaves, he saw a small, swift movement. He blinked. It must have been a bird, he told himself. He didn't know whether he wanted that to be true or not. He edged closer. His blood thrummed in his ears. There it was again. Only this time, he saw it properly. Not a bird. It was the flick of an ear. Through the willow wall he saw a swivelling motion. A great head turned soundlessly towards him. Huge, amber eyes appraised him. Every hair on Brody's skinny arms stood up.

Now that he'd got his eye in, he could clearly see the rest of the tiger stretched out in the shade: the enormous front paws nestled among the leaves the groundsman had cut off, while the back legs lay casually to one side beneath the long, sinuous body, the tail curled round the powerful haunches. A part of Brody's brain marvelled at how camouflaged it was. Its tawny fur ought to have been obvious against the green of the grass and leaves. Yet its stripes made it blend perfectly with the shadows.

He held his breath. In the ten long seconds that followed, a remarkable number of thoughts passed through his head: he considered how much flesh there was on his own body, and weighed this against the possible appetite of the tiger; he recalled a film of a tiger hunting, and tried to work out whether he had any chance of outrunning it, if it should decide on him for dinner; he evaluated the various means of putting distance between him and the animal, trying to decide whether slow and steady would be better than swift and surprising; and lastly, he wondered if anyone was going to come soon enough to rescue him, whether by fighting the tiger off or – more likely – by providing a more appealing meal prospect.

In fact, most of the children were now down at the far end of the playground, drawn by the wails of the Year Three girls who had fled to a safe distance. The staff on playground duty were down there too, attempting to restore calm and establish what had happened, in the face of growing hysteria. Only Mrs Wilson was up at the top of the playground, pinning Carlos Lopez to the fence and shouting at him.

Hearing her, Brody turned his head sideways, not daring to take his eyes off the tiger. "Mrs Wilson!" he whispered as loudly as he could.

She didn't look round. Probably she hadn't heard him over her own strident voice.

Brody looked at the tiger again. It didn't seem especially perturbed by his presence so nearby. He tried a second time, a little louder now. "Mrs Wilson!" He inched away from the willow tunnel, very slowly.

"Not now, Brody!" the supervisor snapped, resuming her attack on Carlos without missing a beat.

Still the tiger didn't move, except for the ear which flicked again. Brody wished it wasn't watching him so intently. He began to glide backwards as smoothly as he could, still moving much less quickly than he would have wished.

NOT NOW, BRODY

"Mrs Wilson!" He was a little braver this time. Surely if the tiger wanted to eat him, it would at least have got to its feet.

"Not now, Brody!" she snarled. "Can't you see I'm busy?"

Brody winced. Would her aggression be enough to rouse the tiger? He couldn't really see it from where he was. The leaves were too thick and the animal's camouflage too good. He didn't think it had stirred, but it was possible.

"Mrs Wilson!" he called, one more time, braver now that he wasn't quite so close.

This time, she turned her head to look at him. "Not. Now. Brody!" Her eyes flashed.

Alright, Brody thought. A few more steps brought him to the edge of the playground, where he went and stood a short distance from the supervisor, waiting for her to finish tongue-lashing Carlos.

He was putting Mrs Wilson off her stride, however. A few seconds later, she let Carlos go with an ominous, "Don't think that's the end of it! I'll finish with you later!" and whirled round on Brody.

"What is it? It had better be good! I don't like being interrupted when I'm dealing with naughty children!"

Brody opened his mouth to speak. For a moment, no words came out: the tiger encounter and Mrs Wilson's rage seemed to have combined to lock his throat. He coughed.

"There's a tiger in the willow tunnel," he said, pleased with how calm he sounded.

"Not you as well!" roared Mrs Wilson. "Those stupid Year Three girls were screaming the place down. I'm surprised at you, Brody Milne, joining in with that kind of nonsense! The children at this school are all such liars!"

"We're not lying!" Even though he'd expected this reaction, Brody felt his cheeks flush. It took some effort to get his voice level again. "If you don't believe us, why don't you go and see for yourself?"

"I will!" Mrs Wilson spun on her heel and stomped

off up the field to the tunnel.

  The most notable event of the year – and of the village's eleven hundred year history – reached its climax on the field of St Andrew's Primary School with all the children inside, safely behind the glass.

  The teachers, realising that no work was going to get done this afternoon, had allowed the older children to gather in the two classrooms that overlooked the grass. Even the headteacher was there. Brody thought he looked more relaxed than usual, despite the gruesome scene being played out before their eyes. The younger children, meanwhile, were drawing tigers in their classrooms, and one little boy had added a stick figure lady with curly hair walking towards it.

  By the time the emergency services arrived, it was much too late for Mrs Wilson. The police officers who were first on the scene kept the fire officers and ambulance crews behind the gates until armed back-up could arrive, though the tiger was far too happily occupied with devouring its kill to take any notice of them at all.

  Brody was sad to learn later that the tranquilliser

dart used by the zoo staff to take the animal away had been lethal rather than a sedative. Apparently, the tiger had got noticeably more aggressive since a boy had poked it in the ear with a stick. This latest incident would have given it a taste for human blood which, given the success of its escape from the zoo in the first place, would have made it a menace.

As for the menace that had been Mrs Wilson, one child from each class went to her funeral. Brody was glad he wasn't chosen, because he got an afternoon off with everyone else. He was also glad because it would have been so hard to keep quiet when everyone said, as they were bound to, that Mrs Wilson was really very nice. Brody couldn't help wondering whether the tiger would have agreed.

Brief Encounter

I never used to believe in hypnosis, not really. I wanted it to be true, of course, but whenever I saw it on the telly, I always suspected the person who volunteered was just playing along!

If it was me, I can just imagine myself on the stage, listening to them counting and saying, "You are very sleepy, Isobel. Your eyes are very heavy," while I'd be thinking, 'My eyes are fine. I'm not sleepy! Please let me go back to my seat!' But I bet I wouldn't say it. I wouldn't want to let everyone down, especially the hypnotist, because they'd look really bad if everybody knew it hadn't worked. So I can totally see why you might pretend.

In fact, the only way I'd even consider volunteering is if the hypnotist specifically asked for someone who thought they couldn't be hypnotised. I've never heard of that happening, though, so I was blown away when someone visited our school and did exactly that!

Laura Komorowska, or just Laura – she told us not to worry about her Polish surname – was the grown-up daughter of one of our headteacher's friends. She did hypnotism for a living, she explained, and Mrs Newman had invited her to give a demonstration, because she thought we'd find it interesting.

Laura told us how pleased she was to have been asked to visit Lodge Hill Primary. Most of her work was medical, she said, using hypnotism for practical things like helping people stop smoking, or for psychological treatment, helping people recover from scary or upsetting experiences in the past. That could be upsetting for her too, she said, so she loved doing stage hypnosis, because that was always fun.

I liked her straight away. You felt you could trust her, and I knew Mrs Newman wouldn't have invited someone into school who would do anything mean or unfair. So when she asked for a volunteer who thought they couldn't be hypnotised, I put my hand up. I wasn't the only one. Quite a few of us did. I didn't get chosen, and afterwards, I was glad. Who knows what I might have gone and done?

To everyone's frustration, she picked the boy next to me, Max Bowman. As he swaggered up to the front, looking really pleased with himself, I wondered what Laura thought. Had she meant to pick someone like him? I only ask because Max is one of those really annoying kids who's always got their hand up, usually asking something the teacher told us literally thirty seconds before! What's even more annoying is the way he reckons he knows it all, even when he so obviously doesn't. One time, Miss Oliver asked him how many he'd got right in a quiz, and he said twenty-five even though there were only twenty questions!

He thinks he's really handsome, too – he's always running his fingers through his hair, and every time it's own clothes day, he struts round the playground in his latest pair of expensive trainers, expecting everyone to look at him. He reckons he's going to be a film star when he grows up.

The rest of us knew perfectly well that Max had only put his hand up to get attention, not because he actually thought he couldn't be hypnotised. He probably hadn't even listened to what Laura said. In fact, he might be really difficult to hypnotise precisely because he didn't listen!

Laura got him to sit on a chair at the front of the hall. It was facing sideways and there was a clean white-board in front of it. Laura took out a marker pen and drew a black dot in the middle, but nothing else. Then she stood beside it and asked the rest of us to be really quiet because she wanted Max to focus on the dot while she talked.

BRIEF ENCOUNTER

For the first minute or so, he kept stealing looks at the class and rolling his eyes. Laura was very patient. She ignored his smirks and just drew his attention back to the dot again and again.

Meanwhile, we were all watching avidly for any sign that he was starting to get hypnotised. When he'd first sat down, Max had put his shoulders back and sat up straight, like he was challenging Laura to beat him. After a bit though, he did start concentrating on the dot, like she'd asked. Laura talked quietly about how being hypnotised was very like sleepwalking, where you could do many of the things you would usually do, even though you were asleep. She suggested that Max was curious about hypnosis and told him she could show him what it was like if he didn't try to resist. She reassured him that she wouldn't ask him to do anything he wouldn't want, or try and find out his secrets.

After a while, she got to the heavy eyelid bit, saying how tired his eyes must be from staring at the dot all this time. Her voice was really soothing, but his eyes didn't close and I thought maybe he'd been right, and he couldn't be hypnotised. That would be infuriating! He'd be so smug!

Laura wasn't concerned though. She went on smoothly, telling him how heavy his limbs felt, and how nice it was to let the chair hold his weight as he sank into it.

He'd done so well, keeping his eyes focused on the dot, she said, but wouldn't it be a relief to close them? As she talked on, Max's eyes did close.

Laura began to count slowly from one to ten, explaining softly between the numbers how she was helping him to go to sleep. We all leaned forward. Was he pretending? Maybe. I didn't think so, though. His body language had changed: his shoulders had dropped and his hands hung at his sides, making him look a bit like a gorilla. I couldn't believe he'd willingly look so stupid.

"While we do the next few things together," Laura said, "you'll forget all about the other children watching. You'll feel as though there's nobody in the room except you and me, and you'll be keen to impress me by doing the things I ask you as well as you can. Is that alright?"

Max nodded.

"That's lovely. First of all, I'd like you to stand up and put your arms out in front of you with the palms facing each other but not touching. Now, can you feel them pushing each other apart, like magnets repelling each other? I'm sure you can."

Max's hands began to drift away from each other as she spoke.

"That's fantastic," Laura said. "I think they'll go right

91

out until they're stretched out like wings by your sides."

Max did just what she said. I was amazed.

"Now, I want you to imagine you're a seagull gliding across the sky. Open your eyes and soar round the room. Can you feel the wind through your feathers and the thermal updraughts carrying you higher?"

Max nodded again, and began to gallop round the hall, flapping his arms. Several kids started to giggle.

"You're very high up in the sky, looking down on the coastline below," Laura said. "I'm down there, looking up at you, hoping to see you do some acrobatics as you fly!"

In response to this, Max dived at the floor and did a clumsy forward roll. The whole class began to laugh but he didn't seem to hear. He just carried on flying round the room, with another couple of forward rolls and even a rubbish cartwheel, until Laura invited him to come and land in front of her.

"Fold your wings by putting your hands behind your back," she told him.

By now, I was sure she'd successfully hypnotised him. Max wasn't just going along with this! No way! He thought he was seriously cool as well as handsome, so he'd never have behaved like this, especially not in front of the class.

Laura invited him to sit in the chair again, then

pointed at nothing above his head.

"I think that's a mosquito, isn't it?" she said. "Can you hear it whining? Look at the way it's zipping around."

Max's eyes followed the invisible insect, and I tell you, it was the craziest mosquito I've ever not seen!

"Do you think you can swat it?" Laura asked. "It's going to be difficult to get, but maybe if you jump a bit, you'll be able to kill it with the rolled up newspaper you've got in your hand. Quick, before it bites you!"

The class burst out laughing now, as Max leapt out of his chair and jumped about the place, swatting wildly at thin air with his imaginary weapon. I glanced at Miss Oliver. She was chuckling. So was Mrs Newman.

"There!" Laura said. "You got it! Well done!"

Max beamed.

"You can put your newspaper down now. I was wondering, if you were an animal, what animal would you be?"

"A squirrel," Max said promptly.

There was another ripple of laughter from the class.

"How lovely!" Laura said. "Can you show me what you'd be like?"

"Yeah, sure," Max said, and he dropped onto all fours and began to hop along the floor, hands first, then feet. After he'd hopped around a bit, he clearly decided he'd found a nut because he settled back on his haunches, gnawing on an invisible ball he was holding. It looked to be the size of a melon.

Laura smiled. "That's very good, Max! When we finish this hypnosis in a few minutes, you won't remember most of it, but you will remember what a good squirrel you are, and you'll tell that to the first person you speak to."

There was a lot of giggling at that.

"Now, you can stop being a squirrel and turn back into a boy. I'd like you to come and sit in the chair again for the last thing we're going to do."

Max stood up and came back to the chair meekly. It was so strange to see him so completely focused on Laura and so oblivious to the rest of us. He was never like that in the classroom.

"I'm going to ask you a question in a moment," Laura said, "and when I do, you're going to answer it in a really high voice. Okay?"

"Okay," Max squeaked. Everyone laughed, but he still didn't notice.

"Very good. Now, can you tell me something about yourself that people don't know, but you'd actually like everyone to know? Take a moment to think about that if you'd like to. Remember, I'm not asking you to give away your secrets. This should be something you *want* people to know."

Max nodded. Then, in the same squeaky voice as before, he said, "Once, when we went to the zoo, I poked a tiger in the ear with a stick!" He grinned, apparently expecting praise or maybe even applause.

Laura frowned. "Oh dear," she said. "That wasn't a very kind thing to do, was it? I hope the tiger wasn't hurt."

Max's face fell. It looked as though it had only just dawned on him that he might have been cruel to the animal. "I think it was okay," he squeaked, less confidently. "It growled a bit and then got up and wandered off."

"Good. I'm glad. Okay, Max, thank you very –"

"Hang on!" Max squealed. "I haven't finished! There's

something else I want to tell you."

"Oh, right." Laura's tone was guarded now.

"Yes, I found a really clever way of cheating in tests – I pretend to be writing and then I sneak a look at the person's work next to me. It's really funny because the teachers haven't noticed yet!"

Laura's eyebrows went up. "You copy from the person next to you? You think you invented that?" Her lips twitched. "So, are you getting really good marks?"

"No. I've always been sat next to Ben, and he gets lots of things wrong."

"I see." Laura glanced across at Miss Oliver and Mrs Newman. All three of them were clearly trying not to laugh.

"And there's another thing too!" Max squealed enthusiastically. "I always wear pants with the days of the week on – always the right ones for the right day, so that I can remember what day it is."

This was too much for the class. The room erupted into howls of laughter. Laura's mouth fell open. She shook her head. "Thank you for sharing that with me, Max," she said, pulling herself together. "Are you quite sure you wanted me to know that?"

"Yeah, definitely!" he squeaked. "If I was Mrs Newman, I'd make it part of the uniform so that everyone could remember what day it was more easily. In the holidays, I sometimes don't bother to wear trousers so that I can quickly see what day it is. I can't do that at school, so when I need to know, I peep in to check."

"You look inside your trousers at school to see what day of the week it is?" Laura's voice was quivering, as though she might be about to cry.

"That's right. Look, I'll show you today's pair!" He jumped up and started to undo his trousers.

"Stop!" Laura cried. "Stop, Max!" She held up her hand. "You mustn't do anything that might embarrass you later! Imagine you're in the classroom with the other children. You wouldn't want to take your trousers off in front of them, would you?"

Max had paused. Now he shrugged, and finished unzipping his trousers, letting them fall to his ankles.

The class dissolved into a shrieking mass of children. At last, Max seemed to hear us. I thought he'd freeze, but he smiled, as though it was the most normal thing in the world to stand at the front of the room with his trousers around his feet.

"It's fine, Laura," he said to our visitor, still squeaking. He sat down on his chair and tugged off his socks and shoes. "I'm going to be an actor when I grow up, but before I do that, I'm going to do some modelling."

He kicked off his trousers altogether, then pulled his shirt off over his head. "I had a friend called Callum who used to go to this school," he said in his shrill voice. "He said I looked great in my pants. He said I should forget acting and just be a model."

Max stood up and struck a pose. He was wearing nothing but a pair of skimpy little briefs with the word TUESDAY across them!

The hall became a zoo. I laughed so much, my stomach hurt. Around me, there were kids doubled over, kids rolling on the floor. Tears were running down our faces, and there were yelps of hysteria. Meanwhile, Max flounced to and fro, one hand on his hip, whisking round at each end, apparently delighted to have our attention.

Finally, Mrs Newman stood up and clapped her hands. "That's enough now, children!" she said loudly. "It's been great fun, but it's time to stop. Laura needs to bring Max round from his trance."

But it was too late for that. The sudden sound of her hands had clearly jerked Max awake. Confusion flashed across his face. He looked at Mrs Newman, then at Laura, and then at all of us. Over half of the kids were still crying with laughter, and even those of us who'd managed to get a grip were sniggering.

Max looked down at himself and saw his bare chest and limbs, and his Tuesday pants. His gaze took in his clothes and shoes, strewn across the floor. His eyes showed total bewilderment, then horror. I almost felt sorry for him. He'd obviously believed Callum – which was stupid of him, given that Callum got expelled – and imagined the rest of us as an adoring crowd! The reality must be very different from what he'd expected!

"Would you like to get dressed, please, Max?" Mrs Newman said. "You've been a wonderful volunteer. I'm sorry to drag you back to the real world so abruptly."

Max grabbed his clothes and began to scramble into them.

"Are you okay?" Laura asked. She looked a little anxious.

He nodded.

BRIEF ENCOUNTER

"Well done." She turned to face us. "That was a more interesting session than I was expecting," she said, smiling. "You never quite know what's going to happen when you put someone to sleep. I'd like you all please to give Max a round of applause for being such a great volunteer!"

We clapped madly. The worry cleared from Max's face, and he looked pleased. I stopped even thinking about feeling sorry for him. You could practically hear his brain rewriting the memory of this day, to cast himself as the hero and the rest of us as worshipping onlookers.

"Very good. Alright, Max, you can go and sit down."

Max picked his way back through the class to his place next to me. He sat down and looked me in the eye.

Without a shadow of a smile, he squeaked, "I'm a really good squirrel, you know!" and looked utterly dumbfounded as we all wailed with laughter.

Baker's Dozen

Callum didn't like school.

School didn't like Callum much either. St. Mary's was his fourth school in three years. It would be his last, for no better reason than that he was in Year Six now and it was June.

He'd only hung on this long at St. Mary's to get the Year Six trip to London earlier this week, but that had turned out so disappointing! Callum had thought they'd have some free time to look round, but they'd gone from the coach into the museum and then straight back to the coach! Boring!

It definitely hadn't been worth coming to school for, and he wasn't planning on showing up again after today unless he was so bored he really couldn't think of anything else to do. That wasn't likely unless his gaming got stopped, if the electricity or internet got cut off again because Dad hadn't paid the bill. Even if that did happen, he'd probably

101

manage to find someone to hang out with like he always had before.

He was done with primary school. He was done with school full stop. Sure, he was supposed to be going to secondary in September, at least his name was on the list for Edward Merchison Academy, but how long would he last there? He'd always got chucked out from everywhere. It was part of who he was. It had become a bit of a challenge in a way, a sort of battle between him and whichever school had taken him on now. The challenge was to see how bad he had to be before they gave in and expelled him.

Some schools tried harder than others, he'd noticed, while some just rolled over at the first sign of trouble. Secondary might be a bit tougher with their so-called sanctions, but that would probably just mean they'd move to exclusion quicker.

Callum liked it when they got to that point. Everyone was on the same page then. That was when the school stopped pretending he needed extra support in the classroom, or some sort of touchy-feely talking time in a calm space. That was when they gave up nosing through his school records, trying to 'understand what had gone wrong' in the past.

Exclusion meetings were where the school finally got

it: where they finally saw that he'd set fire to the classroom bin because he felt like it (Lodge Hill Primary); where they accepted that he'd mooned at the church inspector because he wanted to wipe the stupid smile off her face (St. Stephen's); or where they realised they should have locked up the school kitchen to stop him getting a knife and slashing the bags in the cloakroom just for the hell of it! That last one had been Friarsgate Junior, and the best fun of all.

St. Mary's hadn't got to that point yet. Callum had tried some of the easy stuff, swearing loudly and repeatedly in the classroom, coming to school in trainers and a hoody, skiving off altogether. But St. Mary's was still at the stage where the teachers were smugly thinking they were managing Callum's behaviour so much better than the previous schools!

After all, he'd volunteered to help with the baking for the cake stall at tomorrow's school fête, hadn't he? That showed he was engaging positively in the school community, didn't it? St. Mary's was going to succeed where the others had failed, and give him a good finish to his primary years. St. Mary's was going to be the springboard for the poor, misunderstood boy to launch himself into successful secondary school life.

Callum knew this was what they were thinking, even

though they hadn't said it: the headteacher, his class teacher, the T.A.s and all the rest. Even the woman who was doing the baking session on behalf of the P.T.A. had picked up on it, and was talking to him in that special voice these people used for keeping everything light and positive. It made Callum snarl inside, but on the outside, he smiled sweetly. He'd be smiling properly tomorrow, laughing out loud in fact, when they discovered what he'd done!

He hadn't done the deed yet, but he'd done all the preparation. His gran's bathroom cupboard had been a gold mine, overflowing with all the different medicines she and Grandad had taken over the years, three quarters of them way out of date! Callum had locked himself in the bathroom and spent a happy half hour going through the boxes and bottles, reading the labels and side-effects, and deciding.

The bottled stuff, he'd realised when he'd got here, would be more trouble than it was worth to try and get into the tiny food colouring bottles. And it was no use putting it in the milk either, because none of the recipes used more than a dash.

He got the powder out instead. That was going to be much easier, and actually, it was the best bet anyway. Callum didn't want to kill anyone, just in case it got traced back to him. He was bound to wind up in prison sooner or later – his older brother had, though he was out at the moment – but you got off much lighter for burglary or drugs than you did for murder. What he'd planned for this weekend shouldn't land him in prison, unless there was some consequence he hadn't thought of. It was just a bit of fun!

He looked down at the recipe print-out on the table next to him. There were twelve kids baking in the cookery room, and each of them was making a different cake or batch of biscuits or cupcakes for the cake stall. Callum was pleased with himself for thinking to put the ground up tablets in a flour bag. That was going to make it so much easier to distribute the powder. The question was how much to put in his own recipe, and whether he would have any spare for any of the other cakes. On the one hand, the more people he could hit, the better! On the other, he didn't want to spread the stuff too thinly, and he kind of wanted them to know it had been him, since he'd be long gone by the time they figured out what he'd done.

The P.T.A. lady buzzed round the room, checking how the children were getting on, helping with weighing and beating, and showing a couple of them how to separate an egg. When she got to Callum, he wasn't very far along. She gave him a sympathetic smile that said – plain as day – that it wasn't surprising, was it? He probably hadn't ever baked a cake in his life, poor boy!

Callum's face was starting to feel like it might split from the smile he'd stuck on it. Stupid cow! He knew well enough what he was doing! You didn't have to be a genius to follow a recipe, even if it was a bit more precise than the cooking he did at home, when Dad was working late and it was down to him to feed himself and his sister.

"You seem to have two bags of flour here," the P.T.A. woman said, putting her head on one side and giving what she probably thought was a silvery laugh.

"I noticed there wasn't much in this one," Callum said, holding up the powder bag, "so I thought I'd finish it off before I start on the next one."

"Good thinking!" She hovered over him. Callum beat the margarine and sugar harder, hoping she would move on.

"Time for the eggs, don't you think?"

Callum broke the eggs into a bowl and tipped them into the mix.

"That's looking lovely! Well done!" Still she lurked.

Callum's smile slipped. Patronising old bag! 'Well done!' he mimicked silently, bending over the mixture and pretending it was her face he was battering with the wooden spoon.

"Shall we sift the flour in?" Without waiting for his reply, she picked up the sieve and poured his bag of powdered tablets into it. Callum gulped. He hoped he'd ground them all up fine enough. The stuff did look quite like flour and there were no obvious fragments in it. Even so, it didn't smell right. Before the P.T.A. woman could notice, he poured real flour from the second bag over the top and added the cocoa. It was just as well he hadn't been set on sharing the powder around, he thought irritably.

"I'll carry on from here, shall I?" he said. "I do know what I'm doing."

The woman nodded. "Are you going to do cupcakes or one large cake?"

Callum considered. Whole cakes sometimes didn't get finished, yet you never saw a cupcake left on a cake stall. If he wanted to be sure the whole lot would go ... "Cupcakes."

"Good. I'll find you a tray and some paper cases while you finish off the mix."

The woman left him alone after that, much to Callum's relief. He filled the cupcake cases with mixture and put them in the tray. There were only twelve holes but he had thirteen cakes. Never mind, he thought, and put the extra one on the oven shelf beside the tray.

When they came out fifteen minutes later, they were brown and fluffed up and beautiful. Callum grinned. Even without any icing, they looked delicious. You'd definitely never guess there was anything unusual about them. He spread them out to cool and then began applying the icing in swirls and twirls, stars and flowers. He'd looked this up on the internet and practised, having borrowed an icing bag and nozzles from the old lady in the flat downstairs. It was the guaranteed way of making sure the cakes were chosen first and eaten straight away.

They were spectacular when he'd finished. Callum couldn't help a twinge of pride. The headteacher, Miss Trenton, paused in front of them when she came to inspect the children's efforts just before the bell rang for the end of school.

"You made these, Callum?" she asked, entirely failing to hide her astonishment.

"Yes, Miss," he said. He sensed his smile twist itself towards glee and tried to bring it under control.

Miss Trenton glanced at the P.T.A. woman.

"It's true. They were all his own work," the woman confirmed.

"Except the flour, Miss," Callum pointed out. "You put in the first lot of flour."

The woman simpered. "That was nothing! You did all the rest, including this amazing icing!"

Callum bowed his head modestly and didn't say

anything. It hadn't exactly been nothing that the P.T.A. woman had done!

"They look absolutely marvellous!" Miss Trenton said, beaming. "In fact, I really think you ought to have one yourself as a reward, Callum! We've got plenty to sell, and it seems a shame for you not to get the benefit of all your hard work."

Callum's smile faltered on his lips. He shook his head, straining to appear natural. "I couldn't, Miss!" he protested. "It wouldn't be right! I made them for the cake stall, to raise money for St. Mary's. The P.T.A. deserves to make as much as they can tomorrow."

Miss Trenton's cheeks glowed with pleasure. How much this boy had improved in just a few weeks! "That's so thoughtful of you, Callum! You're quite right. I tell you what, I'll pay for one right now with my own money, so you can have a cake, and the P.T.A. doesn't lose out. Look, you've made thirteen anyway – a baker's dozen! Twelve for the sale, and one for you." She dug around in her pocket and handed some coins to the P.T.A. woman. "Which one would you like?"

Callum could see he had no choice. He scrutinised them all, hoping there was one smaller than the others, or one that might magically have less of the powder in it.

BAKER'S DOZEN

There wasn't.

"I know, I know!" Miss Trenton agreed. "They all look so wonderful! How about that one?" She pointed out one on the right. Callum took it slowly.

"There, well done! Eat up now. I'm sure the others will go like hot cakes tomorrow!"

Callum only just made it home from school in time, running all the way because he knew what was coming. From the last bite in the cookery room to the bathroom at the flat was twelve minutes, and he nearly didn't get there. For the next hour, he didn't dare get off the loo, even though it felt like there was nothing left inside him after the first ten minutes.

He had to lie to his mates about why he couldn't go out with them that evening – if he told them the truth he'd never hear the end of it – and even the following afternoon, the thought of being more than thirty seconds away from a loo felt horribly risky. He didn't know whether laxatives were always like that, or whether the cupcake had delivered an unusually large dose.

He hadn't planned to go to the school fête anyway, so he lay on the couch, gunning down other players on his game and happily imagining the people who'd bought his cakes running for the loos at school. If any of the smaller kids ate one, they probably wouldn't even get out of the school hall in time!

Callum never went back to St. Mary's, of course, so it was almost a month before he found out what had actually happened on the day of the fête. Apparently, Miss Trenton's dog had raced into the cookery room while the P.T.A. was setting up, and had knocked Callum's box of cakes on the floor and wolfed them all down. The explosive mess the dog made, almost instantaneously, was like nothing anyone had ever seen before, including people with a dog of their own, and nobody could face going in to retrieve the rest of the cakes. So there was no cake stall that year.

For her part, Miss Trenton was horrified by what her dog had done, but oblivious to the true cause. On the last day of school at the end of July, she was still regretting Callum's failure to return to St. Mary's. Such a talented baker! She'd been thinking of talking to him about Junior Bake Off. Ah well. Perhaps baking might yet be his path to success out there in the big, wide world.

Firefly

Oscar often daydreamed that he had some sort of superpower. He'd never admitted this to anyone, because daydreaming about superpowers was for young kids, not for a Year Six. Yet, he sat in class quite often imagining himself taking off from the floor and flying away out of the window while everyone gazed after him with awe and envy.

'Dreamy' was a word that had been used to describe Oscar by more than one teacher. He'd heard his mother use it, too. From the way the adults said it, and the fond smiles, they obviously didn't consider it a bad thing. Oscar wasn't quite so sure. It sounded a bit feeble to him; you'd never describe someone powerful as 'dreamy'. 'Dreamy' was more like fairies, wafting about in the breeze.

Still, it was better than what his current teacher had said about him recently, which was 'lazy'. Mum had come back from Parents' Evening surprised and dismayed. Had something changed? she'd asked Oscar. Had something happened to stop him joining in with the rest of the class? 'Joining in with what?' Oscar almost said. Joining in with sitting in silence, copying grammatical structures off the board. Joining in with pages and pages of sums.

School hadn't been like that when Mrs Rose taught them. She'd managed to find fun ways of teaching even the boring stuff. She'd got them to take it turns presenting things to the class, and given them the chance to debate stuff that was in the news. There had been music on at certain times of day, and a daily joke, and they'd done all kinds of really cool art. Unfortunately, however, Mrs Rose had left to have a baby.

The man who was teaching them now – Mr Flight – was like no teacher Oscar had ever come across in real life. He seemed to have marched straight out of the pages of an old-fashioned book about a boys' boarding school: he smelled of pipe tobacco and always wore a suit with a waistcoat, and a jacket made out of that chequered material posh people wore to go shooting. You could practically see your face in his shoes and you could hear him coming a mile off, clipping along the corridors of Friarsgate Junior. His eyebrows were like birds nesting on his craggy face, and his mouth was a rocky outcrop, worn down at both ends by years of disapproval. The only things missing from his schoolmaster costume were a bat-like gown and a cane. Oscar felt sure that Mr Flight would love to be allowed a cane.

He couldn't believe any parents from his class had received a positive report about their child on Parents' Evening. In that, at least, Mr Flight was fair: he disliked all the children in the class equally, and probably all children everywhere. When Oscar tried to say this to Mum though, she got irritated and told him he needed to pull his socks up. Mr Flight's job was to get Year Six ready for secondary school, she said, and that was bound to mean stricter discipline and more formal learning.

What it actually meant for Oscar was more daydreaming. Recognising that Mr Flight wasn't going to give him any credit for the work he did do, he scaled back his efforts to 'bare minimum'. It had been unfair of Mr Flight to describe him as lazy before, but now he definitely was. It served Flighty right, Oscar thought. If Mr Flight was going to make unreasonable accusations, he might as well live up to them, or rather, down to them.

So while his marks plummeted, the amount of time Oscar spent rambling through his own mind expanded marvellously. The daydreams themselves grew more and more elaborate, generally focussed these days on ways of getting revenge on Mr Flight. Some of them were quite inspired, Oscar felt.

There were several variations on pinning the teacher to the wall, floor or even ceiling with laser beams that shot from Oscar's fingers. Sometimes these finished with him whirling the man round with the tip of the beam and flinging him into outer space. Sometimes, Oscar simply vaporised Mr Flight, to roars of approval from the rest of the class. On a bad day, when Mr Flight had been especially cutting, he imagined using his laser like a burner or a scalpel, to score spectacles and a moustache across the teacher's glaring face – prior to vaporising him again.

Alternative scenarios saw Oscar tracking down Mr Flight at home and calling up a band of hags and trolls to invade his house and finish him off; or summoning an alien spaceship to beam him up and away forever. Regrettably,

Oscar was interrupted in the middle of devising torture methods for the aliens to use on Mr Flight, and couldn't quite get back into this daydream again.

There were more humdrum options, too, which achieved their ends without the use of superpowers, trolls, or extra-terrestrials. One of these involved the police turning up and arresting Mr Flight on suspicion of murdering a former pupil. This seemed so plausible to Oscar, he found himself half waiting for it to happen. Then there was one where a different former pupil – not the murdered one – planted a bomb under Mr Flight's car, which blew him up on his way to school.

Musing on the subject of doing away with Mr Flight at home, Oscar daydreamed about posting his great-aunt's boa constrictor through Mr Flight's letterbox. That mightn't be very reliable though, if the snake wasn't hungry enough, or Mr Flight wasn't sufficiently appetising.

A firebomb would be better. Oscar got as far as wondering how you might make a firebomb, but he didn't dare look it up on the internet. The police would be able to trace you afterwards if you did that. And even if you never actually made the thing, the search would be in your internet history forever, no matter how carefully you tried to delete it. That could get you into terrible trouble later on for something you hadn't done.

Oscar wasn't sure he wanted to kill Mr Flight anyway. Even if he got away with it, he'd still have a man's blood on his hands for the rest of his life, which probably wasn't a great start to adulthood. All the same, his final months at Friarsgate would be immeasurably improved if Flighty was gone.

Over time, Oscar increasingly found himself daydreaming about fire. A fire could be easily started, and there were lots of materials readily accessible. As far as Oscar understood, it wasn't too hard to disguise either. He'd seen news reports about electrical fires that had started when a wire got damaged and sparked. Something like that had been enough to burn down half of that cathedral in Paris, hadn't it? An incident like that wouldn't necessarily be traced back to him.

If the whole school burnt down, none of the children would be able to come to classes for a while, which would mean no Mr Flight. On the other hand, that wasn't very specific, and it would cause Mrs Downing, the headteacher, a lot of grief. Mrs Downing was nice, so that would be a shame. He wondered if he could maybe set fire to the classroom in a way that made it look like Mr Flight's fault, so that Mrs Downing fired him.

At this point, Oscar burst out laughing at his own pun, in the middle of the silent classroom.

"What is the matter with you, Grately?" barked Mr Flight from the front.

Oscar stifled his laugh behind a cough. 'Grately' was him. That was another thing about Mr Flight – he called all the boys by their surnames. Did any other junior school teacher anywhere do that these days?

"Nothing, Sir," he mumbled. "I had a frog in my throat."

Mr Flight's eyebrow arched. "I'm expecting at least a full A4 side for this essay," he said. "You don't seem to have written more than a couple of lines. I imagine you don't want to lose your breaktime?"

"No, Sir."

"Well, then, you'd better look sharp!"

Oscar turned his attention to the page he was writing, then glanced across at Farhad's page next to him. Farhad was a lot further on. Oscar tried surreptitiously to read what he'd written.

"Your own, original work, Grately!" Mr Flight flexed a ruler and let it snap against the table.

Oscar sighed and scratched his head while he tried to think what to put next. He tended to muddle up the Mayans and the Aztecs, so comparing either of those civilisations with Britain in the same historical period was always going to be a tall order. He attempted to apply himself.

When a fire did break out at Friarsgate Junior School not long after this, Oscar's first thought was that maybe he had done it somehow. He didn't remember setting light to anything on that evening, not at home and still less at school. But could his superpower daydreams have come true somehow?

Had he done it in his sleep perhaps? He knew it was incredibly unlikely, but he still wondered if he'd sleepwalked to school in the middle of the night, armed with matches and firelighters, or whatever. Was it possible that he'd broken in and started the blaze without remembering any of it? He couldn't really believe it, but he couldn't shrug off the feeling of guilt either. He'd considered starting a fire just like this. He'd wanted it to happen! It must be his fault somehow or another.

There was no school for the rest of the week, even though the newer buildings had escaped damage. The place was crawling with health and safety people, insurance assessors, and a fire investigation team picking minutely through the wreckage. Oscar found himself waiting nervously to hear what they had to say.

As the news trickled out, by rumour at first rather than announcement, it didn't immediately make him feel better. The fire had been started on purpose, they said. The lead fire investigator was certain that it was arson, not an accident or an electrical fire. Oscar wondered how she could be so sure. How had the evidence not got burned away?

When the full statement came, however, he was able to breathe easily again. The fire hadn't started in his classroom. It had begun in the same part of the school, the oldest bit, but it had been in one of the Year Five classes along the corridor from Year Six. Oscar wished he'd found that out sooner. That made it much less likely that he'd done it.

What made him totally sure, though, was the news that the fire alarms had apparently been tampered with. At last, he could enjoy the developments as much as all the other children from Friarsgate. He unquestionably hadn't done anything to the fire alarm system. He didn't even know where in the school it was.

Someone did, though, the fire investigator said, and that person was unlikely to be a child. Moreover, there had been three similar fires in schools elsewhere in the county over the last five years. This time, they had a potential suspect, somebody they were hoping to link to the other arson attacks.

School started back on Monday, and Mrs Downing had a meeting for everyone in the hall to explain what would happen. They must all be patient, please, she said, until everything could get back to normal. For now, all the classes would have to double up to make space for Years Five and Six while that part of the school was rebuilt. To make things easier, there would be small groups working in the library and the hall, and on the field, too, for the rest of the year.

Oscar thought that sounded like fun. Much, much better than that, though, was the news that Mr Flight was off work for some reason. The other Year Six teacher had agreed to teach both classes for the remainder of the school year. Miss Howden was lovely, and Oscar felt as though things couldn't get any better.

A week later, however, they did. An arrest had been made.

FIREFLY

The case didn't come to trial for over a year. By that time, Oscar and his classmates had moved on to secondary school, and the middle months of Year Six were no more than a bad memory. Even so, Oscar cut out the report of the trial from the newspaper and kept it.

Leonard Flight, 68, has been found guilty today of deliberately starting the fire that burned down part of Friarsgate Junior School in May 2018. The jury took less than fifteen minutes to reach a unanimous verdict.

Flight, who lives alone, was briefly a pupil at Friarsgate in 1960, before being thrown out for disruptive behaviour. After Friarsgate, he attended and was expelled from a number of other schools in the area where fires have also broken out in recent years. On leaving school at 14, he joined the army, where he had a successful career as an explosives and incendiary specialist.

When he retired from the forces, he managed to find work as a teacher, despite having no training or qualifications. Fake references enabled him to find work in schools, without any classroom experience except his own unhappy childhood. His sole aim, the judge said, was to return to the classrooms where he'd been humiliated, and exact his revenge.

Flight is believed to be the arsonist behind at least four other fires. The police were able to prove he had started the fire at Friarsgate Junior after he dropped the tin in which he kept his pipe tobacco as he fled the scene. Fingerprints on the tin matched a print inside the fire alarm cupboard.

Further prosecutions are pending.

Oscar pinned the report to his noticeboard. The headline was **FIREFLY TEACHER CRASH AND BURN**. He got out a pen and drew flames around the words. 'Firefly' would have been the perfect nickname for old Flighty, if only they'd known.

He studied the face that glared out of the photograph, then drew spectacles and a moustache on it. As an afterthought, he added a pair of wings and a lightbulb for a tail.

He stood back and admired his handiwork. The pen was all very well, but a laser would have been better! He spread out his fingers in the direction of the noticeboard, and for the very last time, mentally vaporised Mr Flight.

126

Snakes and Ladders

It was no secret that our lovely teacher, Mrs Weller, thought almost all testing was a waste of time. She'd start grumbling about the Year Six SATs in November every year, and by the time they came round in May, she'd apparently be like a storm cloud! I never saw it myself of course, because of what happened, but she was famous for it! She could have changed year groups and taught Year Four or Five, but she always said she loved Year Six, in spite of the SATs.

Fortunately, she didn't blame us for those. She used to say we were in this miserable mess together. According to her, it was the confounded government! (Confounded is a polite way of saying something much ruder, in case you were wondering.) "What planet are they on", she'd cry, "requiring you to know what a fronted adverbial is? No adult in the country has a clue except Key Stage Two teachers!

More to the point, nobody has ever needed to know!" She'd whirl round the room when she said this, her skirts swishing dramatically.

What really used to get to Mrs Weller was the way the confounded government wanted us to stuff our writing with extra adjectives and adverbs, to prove we knew what they were. "If you want to write well," she'd insist, "you should be getting rid of extraneous words, not inserting them!" 'Extraneous' was one of her favourite words. It means 'unnecessary' or 'irrelevant'. Mrs Weller wrote poetry in her spare time, the kind that has almost no text dotted around on an empty page, so she hated extraneous words!

Her least favourite word was probably 'nice'. She herself was very nice, but she'd throw up her hands in despair if she heard me say so! I used the word once – only once – in something I wrote, and she pretty much howled! "There are hundreds of thousands of words in the English language, and you've chosen 'nice'!" I remember her waving her arms around. "I'm disappointed in you! Depressed, discouraged, disgruntled, disillusioned, distressed!" By this point, I was wondering where the tissues were. But then she winked. "Choose your words with care, Alfie! Imagine each one is a gemstone of inestimable worth!" And she gave me one of her electric smiles.

SNAKES AND LADDERS

Mrs Weller wasn't only into literacy, mind you. She did amazing art projects and brilliant science experiments, and she was totally fascinated by the natural world. Whatever topic we were doing for geography, she'd always construct it around wildlife, and she'd even shoehorn nature into history lessons, by teaching us about Darwin's voyages, or getting us to write Victorian newspaper reports about some animal or bird that was hunted to extinction! She owned every TV series David Attenborough had ever made, and each time there was a new one out, we'd watch it in class. Now I think about it, I guess what happened in SATs week made some sense, given she was so crazy about wildlife.

Maybe it had something to do with her retirement, too. I was quite surprised when I found out she was retiring at the end of that school year. Sure, she looked old. But all our teachers looked old except Miss Ingleside, who was middle-aged – twenty six, someone said. I was a bit sorry about Mrs Weller going. I was going to be leaving at the same time so it didn't matter to me, but it meant my sister wouldn't get to have her, which was a shame. When I said that to my mum, she said a year with us lot was enough to make anyone want to retire! My dad muttered something darkly about the new headteacher, but when I asked him what he meant, he backtracked, and said thirty years in teaching was more than enough.

I wondered afterwards if there might be something in what he'd said, about the headteacher, because Mr Johnson seemed to be the one person in the school who didn't love Mrs Weller. Mrs Weller didn't like him either. You could tell because she went all stiff and polite when he came into the classroom. Mr Johnson had only started that January, but his hair was already grey when he arrived, even though his face wasn't wrinkled. Dad reckoned he'd had a breakdown at his last school – some city academy called Haltonbrook – and came here because he thought a country primary school would be an easy ride.

I definitely think he expected us to be easier to bully into shape! He had a proper go! It was always results, results, results, every assembly he did. "The ladder of success is best climbed by stepping on the rungs of opportunity!" he'd cry, sounding weirdly like Adolf Hitler in the film clip we'd watched in class. Quite honestly, I thought he was trying to climb his own ladder of success by stepping on all of us!

I wonder if the reason he didn't like Mrs Weller was to do with her attitude to testing. Mr Johnson was totally the opposite, the sort of man who likes everything to have a number attached to it. Done a fantastic watercolour painting? Give it a mark out of ten! Learnt a new song? Only interested if you can put a percentage on it! I bet he measured the plant in his office every day to record how much it grew!

For a while after he first took over, Mrs Weller did her best to toe the line. It didn't go well. Every time she was trying to show us a new way of doing something, or teaching us something different to what she'd taught before, her face kind of shuttered down.

Then, around Easter, she must have decided to abandon the new stuff, because she went back to what she'd done for the last few years. All of a sudden, she was bright and bouncy and positive again, except for the usual grumbling about the government. In the week before the SATs exams, she was still keeping that up, which another reason you'd never have guessed what was going to happen.

If anyone was going to figure it out, though, it should have been me. I was the first into class on the Monday morning of SATs week, and as I went to get something from my drawer, I saw a large basket in the walk-in cupboard.

"What's that?" I asked. "Is there something in the basket?" It had a lid, held on with leather straps.

A frown flicked across Mrs Weller's face. She closed the cupboard door. "Very observant, Alfie," she said. "You'll find out later. For now, please keep it under your hat."

She must have seen that I looked a bit confused. The basket was tall, like a laundry basket, so it wasn't going to fit under any kind of hat. "Don't tell the others," she said, and smiled. "I can rely on you, can't I?"

I nodded. Naturally, I wanted to ask more, but I dropped the subject because I was flattered that she was trusting me with a secret.

As she took the register a while later, Mrs Weller was unusually cheerful. Given her months of grumbling, I'd

expected her to be specially grouchy now that SATs week was finally here. But she chattered away, making little jokes, for all the world as though she was excited. When Mr Johnson came to give us a last pep talk, and take us through to the hall for the tests, she beamed at him.

The tables had been set out in rows in the hall, spaced out so that you couldn't see anyone else's work. We each sat down at one, in alphabetical order, with a pen, pencil and rubber in front of us, and nothing else.

"As you know," Mr Johnson said, "today is Paper One – grammar, punctuation and vocabulary – followed by Paper Two – spelling." He was opening a package as he spoke. Mrs Weller hadn't followed him into the hall.

Inside the package was a stack of exam papers. Mr Johnson gave them out and then read the instructions aloud. We listened. Mrs Weller still didn't join us. I wondered if Mr Johnson had decided to supervise our tests personally, on his own. Perhaps he thought we'd try harder if he prowled round the room, peering over our shoulders.

"You will have forty five minutes to answer the questions in this booklet," he announced. "You may now start the test."

I turned to the first page and picked up my pen. Before I had a chance to read the questions, however, a movement high up on the wall at the side of the hall caught my eye. Curled around the bars we use for P.E. was the most amazing, bright green snake!

I stared at it. It was hard to say how long it was, because it was all kinked up, but I guessed about two metres. It was stretching out its neck, if snakes have necks.

I glanced at the other kids. Everyone else was looking down at their work. Mr Johnson had his back to the snake as well, so I was the only person who'd noticed it.

Mrs Weller walked into the hall just then. She didn't look at the snake either. Instead, she looked straight at me. Then she raised both eyebrows and made a silent signal to keep quiet. She knew the snake was there, I realised! That was what had been in the basket!

She was carrying an open shoe box, and while Mr Johnson wasn't looking, she put it down on the floor directly underneath the snake, without looking up. Then she walked away, hands behind her back, pretending to patrol the exam hall.

I thought I'd better start work on my test, since it was clear I mustn't draw attention to the snake. It was so hard to concentrate, though! I really wanted to look up and see if it was slithering down the bars.

Then I heard Mr Johnson's footsteps coming along

my row. I kept my head down. When he got to my desk, the footsteps stopped. I glanced up. He was frowning, probably because I hadn't answered a single question. I wanted to explain, but I knew we weren't allowed to talk.

It was almost as though he heard my thought, however, because he turned round, and saw the box down on the floor next to the wall. Strangely, he didn't look up as he walked over to it.

"Oh, really!" The exclamation burst from him as he saw what was inside. He bent to pick it up. At the same moment, someone shrieked.

Then the rest of the class started screaming. Everyone had now seen what Mr Johnson hadn't: the green snake was only just above his head.

The headteacher looked up. His mouth fell open but no sound came out. The snake was looping down and down. Now, it extended itself towards him, keeping the tail end of its body curled around the bars while it stretched out the other end. Its head slid over Mr Johnson's right shoulder and across his chest to his left shoulder. The rest of it followed.

The colour drained from Mr Johnson's face, like someone had taken the plug out in the sink. He stood completely still.

SNAKES AND LADDERS

The snake extended another coil, gliding smoothly around the back of Mr Johnson's neck and over his right shoulder again, encircling his throat completely. The screaming died away as we all held our breath. Was it going to tighten its coils and squeeze?

Mr Johnson swayed. The snake's head tilted as it felt the movement, but it stayed motionless in the air. Then it stretched forward once more, opening its jaws wide. Its teeth were like daggers. For a moment, I thought it was going to bite Mr Johnson before it strangled him!

With a lunge, it struck! Its head vanished into the box he was holding. When it raised it again, its razor teeth were sunk into a dead rat.

Mr Johnson crumpled to the floor, unconscious. The snake retreated with the rat, withdrawing its coils from the headteacher's throat and winding its way up the bars once more. There was a moment of dumbfounded silence. Then chaos broke out. Children shrieked, shouted and wailed. There was laughter, chatter and crying. I looked around. Some of the kids were standing on their chairs. Next to me, Leo was hiding underneath his!

Mrs Weller was crossing the hall. Her face was a little pale, though not the deathly white of Mr Johnson's. She bent down and put her fingers to his pulse. I heard her breath whistle out. She straightened up again. In her eyes was an expression that might have been satisfaction. She clapped her hands.

"Stop the noise, please, everyone. You don't want to frighten the snake, especially while its eating."

The class shut up instantly.

"Does anyone know what kind of snake this is?" Mrs Weller asked. She sounded completely calm.

There was a quiet sob from one of the girls.

"Come along," she said. "We saw this on Attenborough."

I put my hand up. "Is it an emerald tree boa?"

She smiled. "Very good, Alfie. And what do we know about boas?"

A girl called Melody put up her hand. "They're not venomous. They're constrictors. They squeeze their prey to death."

Mrs Weller nodded. "Well done, Melody. That's right."

"Was it trying to squeeze Mr Johnson to death?" Thomas called out.

"Yeah! It was wound right round his neck!"

"I thought he was a dead man!"

"Is he dead?"

Mrs Weller shook her head. "Mr Johnson has passed

out, but he's absolutely fine. He was much too big for Rodrigo to take on! Rodrigo just wanted his rat."

"How do you know it's called Rodrigo?"

"Is it your snake?"

"Wasn't the rat already dead?"

Mrs Weller ignored the first two questions. "They come frozen, and then you thaw them out," she said. "That'll be enough to keep Rodrigo going for three weeks, so you can imagine, Mr Johnson would have been way too big for him to eat!" The corners of her mouth twitched.

"Now," she went on, "I'm afraid this disruption means you can't possibly continue the test – your results wouldn't be a fair assessment at all. What a shame Rodrigo interrupted us like this! I'd brought him in to show you after the tests, as a treat, but he must have got out when I wasn't looking."

She glanced down at Mr Johnson again. "Evie, please go to the office and ask them to call an ambulance. Tilly, lead the way back to the classroom. You can all leave everything where it is on the tables. Alfie, fetch me Rodrigo's basket, please."

I grinned. While everyone else milled around, brave now that the snake was back at the top of the bars, happily engaged with his rat, I nipped back to the classroom.

SNAKES AND LADDERS

When I got back to the hall with the basket, Mrs Weller wasn't there, however. Rodrigo had managed to get his jaws all the way round the rat, and had a rat-shaped lump in his throat. There was no sign of him coming down. I put the basket on the floor beside the climbing bars and waited. Mrs Weller didn't come.

After about five minutes, I decided I'd misunderstood, and went back to the classroom. She wasn't there either, but she came in behind me, looking slightly flustered and shoving her car keys into her pocket.

We never did do the rest of the SATs tests, not that day nor during the rest of the week. The deputy head said she was sure Mr Johnson would have put the test papers in the safe in his office, but they were nowhere to be found. Perhaps he'd taken them home, she said – exams were very important to him, after all! Nobody could ask him, though, because he was in hospital, quite unwell.

Year Six spent the rest of that Monday morning scooting in and out of the hall to see if Rodrigo was ready to come down. By lunchtime, there was no further movement, so the catering staff decided to serve the children in their classrooms. Despite Mrs Weller's assurances that Rodrigo was quite harmless, nobody felt happy about having the whole school in the hall with a two metre long snake.

In the afternoon, Mrs Weller suggested we push together the tables that had been set out for our tests, and start work on a huge piece of wall-art featuring Rodrigo. I found some emerald green pastels, and we painted the rainforests of South America around him, as though he was in his native habitat. We added some poison dart frogs and a scarlet macaw for extra colour. When it was finished, which took half of SATs week, it really was awesome! Mrs Weller put it up in the corridor outside Year Six, and took a picture so she'd have something to remember us all by.

I joked that she should print out a copy and send it to Mr Johnson as a get well card. She laughed, so I didn't think she'd taken me seriously. I heard later she had, though. Maybe that was what pushed him over the edge, because he never came back, not even in September when Mrs Weller and Rodrigo were safely out of the way, enjoying her retirement!

And they definitely were enjoying it, too! The following May, when my sister's Year Six class was about to sit their SATs tests, Mrs Weller emailed them a picture of her with Rodrigo. They were in Brazil, beside the Amazon, because she was hoping to release him into the wild. She'd never meant to own a snake like that, she'd told us that Monday. It wasn't right. She only had him because she'd found him curled up in her garage after someone had dumped him.

She'd been up on a step ladder when she'd first glimpsed him. I thought that was poetic. The step-ladder had been Mrs Weller's ladder of success! Or was it that Rodrigo had been her snake of success? I couldn't decide. Rodrigo meant different things to different people: he was undoubtedly Mr Johnson's downfall, just like in the board game.

It wasn't all over for Mr Johnson, though. After he got out of hospital, he started his own business, working from home, making hand-built ladders. Nobody's seen him out and about much, because he can't stand anything bright green – so grass is traumatic – and he has a phobia of anything long and thin, which includes tape and string. Apparently, the guys who made Pirates of the Caribbean contacted him because they needed a specially long rope ladder for another film, but just the thought of it was enough to send him back to bed for three weeks!

He's on the mend again now, I heard. He's hoping to get into the Guinness Book of Records for 'ladder with most rungs'! I wasn't sure that was a thing, but maybe it is. Whatever, I'd like to be the first to wish him every success with that. The 'ladder of success' built from the 'rungs of opportunity'! I'm sure Mrs Weller will be super happy for him too, when the news reaches her and Rodrigo in Brazil!

With love from Brazil ♡

Teacher's Pet

Inside the cleaning cupboard at Haltonbrook Primary Academy was another, half-hidden cupboard. It wasn't a small cupboard you might naturally overlook, but a full-size, walk-in one. Yet, as far as Ria could tell, not many people knew it was there, and nobody seemed to know what was in it. It was locked, double locked really, since the outer door was usually kept locked too.

Ria discovered the cupboard when she found the outer door open one lunchtime and looked in. The shelves on either side were stacked high with cleaning materials and lightbulbs, and there was a hoover and a floor polisher, and a couple of ladders. She was just turning away when she heard a strange scraping noise.

She peered into the cleaning cupboard again, and only then noticed the door at the back of it. A rack of brooms and mops had been screwed onto the door. The noise was coming from behind it.

Curious, she shimmied between the hoover and

polisher. There was a tiny round hole in the door at about the height of Ria's forehead. She stood on tiptoe and put her eye to it, but she couldn't see anything. She tried the door. It didn't open. The noise had stopped. What could it have been? she wondered. It was quite a particular sound, and not one she could easily place. And why did the door have a separate lock?

The next time she saw Mr Stamp, the caretaker, she asked him about the hidden cupboard. He said he didn't know what was in there. He didn't have the key. Nobody did, he thought, which Ria found rather odd. Later, when she discovered what was behind that door, she shuddered to think how close she'd been. What if the handle had turned when she'd tried it? Might it have been her instead of Darius?

In fact, Ria was almost as close to the cupboard when she sat at her desk in the classroom. She'd worked out that it must be on the other side of the wall, and she was trying to visualise the school from above, and estimate how big the space might be, as she sat in her Friday afternoon science lesson.

Her musings were interrupted by the teacher's voice. "Ria? Do you know?" Mr Rosenthal was staring at her from behind his tinted spectacles.

Ria tried not to look blank. "Is it stamen?" she guessed, glancing at the board.

Mr Rosenthal rubbed his forehead with his pale fingers. His nails were too long. They gave Ria the creeps. The way she caught him looking at her sometimes was creepy too, with a calculating expression, as though he were trying to guess her weight or something.

"You weren't listening, Ria," he said coldly. "I asked what the stamen are for."

Ria blushed and mumbled something about pollen,

and was relieved when his gaze moved on to Darius.

Darius seemed to be the new favourite, Ria noticed. Last year, it had been Josh Ramirez in the glare of Mr Rosenthal's attention, but he'd left rather suddenly. Now, it was Darius Ahmadi in the spotlight. When Ria thought about it afterwards, she could see that it was around this time Darius began to change.

Darius was the class comedian, loud and cocky. He was handsome and knew it, and he might be bright too, but he was so lazy it was hard to tell. Ria had the impression he thought it wasn't worth making an effort for anything or anyone because he was bound to do well in life regardless. This annoyed her deeply, all the more so because she knew he was probably right. One thing was certain: he definitely wasn't the type of kid to be a teacher's pet. Even if he had been, nobody in their right mind would be a teacher's pet to someone like Mr Rosenthal.

He was weird, Mr Rosenthal, if you could use that word without accidentally making him sound interesting. He wasn't. Ria was sure every single child at Haltonbrook found him achingly dull. As far as she knew, he wasn't married, and he definitely didn't have children of his own – unless he'd bored them to death! She supposed he lived alone, but what he did when he wasn't in school, she

146

couldn't imagine. Played the organ, maybe. That would fit.

Although he'd worked at Ria's school for a couple of years, he wasn't a class teacher. Instead, he moved between classes, filling in when other teachers were away on courses or off sick, and teaching science to all the pupils and German to the older ones.

'Teaching' felt like an overstatement of what he did, though. It wasn't really teaching. He talked. Nobody listened. Even if it did count as teaching, it certainly wasn't learning. It was a pity, Ria thought. She had the feeling that science could be interesting. Maybe it would be at secondary school. For now, though, they were stuck with the dullest teacher on the planet!

The first inkling Ria had, that there might be more to Mr Rosenthal than met the eye, was when she realised that his car hardly ever left the staff car park. She'd happened to walk past school several times in the Christmas holidays, and the same blue Vauxhall was always there, even on Boxing Day when the school was all dark and clearly locked up. Her friends shrugged when she mentioned it, but Ria found herself keeping an eye on that car.

She wasn't sure who it belonged to until one evening in January, when she was on her way back from cricket practice. It was about eight o'clock, and the blue Vauxhall

147

was just swinging into the school car park with Mr Rosenthal at the wheel. What was he doing, coming back here at this time? True, the lights were on in the hall, probably for a judo class or a Weight Watchers meeting, but he couldn't be going to either of those. He was so thin, he'd surely snap if you threw him down on a mat!

She might have forgotten all about it, but not long after, he didn't turn up for their Friday afternoon lesson. It was the second time this had happened. Last time, Darius had gone to look for him, Ria remembered. Darius wasn't in school today, and actually, Ria realised, he might not have jumped at the chance to get out of the classroom this time. He was quieter these days, scarcely ever cracking jokes or acting up. He'd lost some weight too, and there was a glassy look to his eyes, especially during Mr Rosenthal's lessons.

Ria volunteered to go and look for Mr Rosenthal, not because she wanted to find him – she decidedly didn't – but because his absence had reawakened her curiosity about him.

"He must be in the building somewhere," Mrs Hunter in the school office told her. "He was here before lunch, and I haven't seen him go out. Have you tried the staffroom?"

Ria went to the staffroom. Ms Young, the Year Three teacher, opened the door to her. "No, he's not here," she

148

said. "He never comes to the staffroom."

"Really?" Ria was surprised. "Not even at break times or when he isn't teaching?"

Ms Young shook her head. "I assume he eats his lunch in the car. He obviously prefers to keep himself to himself. I don't think I've ever seen him in here."

Ria frowned. The part about keeping himself to himself made sense, but she'd never seen him anywhere near his car except that once, certainly not at break or lunch.

"Can I check the staff toilets?" Ria said.

"Go round all the classrooms first, and the library, and if you still haven't found him then yes, check the loos."

Ria did. When she got as far as the loos, she pushed the door open slowly. The last thing she wanted was to find him halfway through hitching his trousers up! There was no sign of Mr Rosenthal there either, though. Oh well, she thought, maybe we'll get to do art instead of having him.

She went back to the classroom, but at the door, she heard feet behind her. She turned round to see Mr Rosenthal hurrying after her, even paler than usual. His eyes were bleary behind his glasses and his hair was dishevelled.

"There you are, Sir!" she said. "I was sent to look for

you."

"I know, I know!" The teacher was plainly agitated. "I over- " He broke off abruptly. "That is, I overran, on the phone. I had a telephone meeting. Very important."

Ria smiled politely, waiting at the door of the classroom for him to catch her up. As he reached her, however, he reeled back. He threw one arm across his face and doubled over, gagging.

"Are you okay, Mr Rosenthal?" She put out a hand to touch his shoulder, but withdrew it quickly. Cold seemed to come off the surface of his shirt.

He straightened up and backed away, warding her off with the other hand. "What did you have for lunch?" he gasped.

His question was so unexpected, Ria giggled. "Spaghetti bolognese," she said.

"What else?"

"Er ... Chocolate pudding ... um, and some salad."

"That can't be it! What else?"

Ria was momentarily at a loss. Then she remembered. "Oh yes, garlic bread."

"Garlic bread!" Mr Rosenthal almost shrieked. "I wish they wouldn't do garlic bread!" He flapped his hand urgently at Ria. "Go on! Go on in!"

Ria went into the classroom, leaving him to follow. What an odd conversation! she thought. First the disappearance, then the lie about where he'd been – she was sure he'd been asleep – and then this bizarre reaction to the lunch menu!

The evenings by now were getting slowly lighter. Mr Rosenthal's car still didn't seem to leave the car park, and Ria didn't see him before lessons, or after school, or around the school generally like the other teachers. She was baffled by this, but her friends insisted there must be a reasonable explanation. Maybe Mr Rosenthal lived in the block of flats at the end of the road, and had permission to keep his car at school. Maybe he nipped home on foot for lunch.

One late afternoon, just after sunset, as Ria and her brother were walking the dog over the school playing field, she noticed a little window propped open at the back of the building. It was fairly high off the ground, and too small for a person to climb in or out of, even a child, which must be why it could be left open when the school was closed. It was a little way along from her own classroom window.

As she was thinking about this, a dark shape dropped

out of the window and then soared up and away through the sky. Was it a bird? she wondered. The flight wasn't right. It was too big for an insect, even a large moth. No, it must have been a bat. That was it! Quite a big bat, in fact! What was a bat doing inside school?

She paused on the path. Since the window was next to her classroom, it must open from the cupboard inside the cupboard. She hadn't noticed it before, but it had obviously always been there. If it had always been open too, bats might well have decided to roost inside, happily undisturbed.

She wondered about going home to get a ladder and torch so she could have a look; but it was quite a walk, and her parents wouldn't much like it. Besides, if there really were a load of bats in there, she didn't want them flying out in her face because she'd woken them up with the torchlight!

She ran to catch up with her brother, aware of a faint feeling of unease. There wasn't exactly anything wrong, but Ria couldn't shrug off the sense that she was staring at the pieces of a puzzle, unable to see how they fitted together. It

was only a couple of days later that the puzzle fell into place in her head. By then, it was much, much too late for Darius.

Once Ria knew the truth, it was so obvious, she couldn't believe she hadn't worked it out before! Had she known at some level, deep down in her mind? Had she simply not dared face it? Or had she stopped her brain from fully forming the thought, because it was so far-fetched? Yet, half the evidence at least was right there, in front of her eyes: first Josh had left, gone home one Wednesday and not come back; and then Darius had changed. From being the kid whose personality filled the classroom, he'd become subdued, withdrawn even. By the time she saw him tap on the cleaning cupboard door and step inside, he was a shadow of his earlier self.

Had Mr Rosenthal chosen him for his olive skin? Was he thinking that the puncture marks wouldn't show up as badly as on white skin? Or had he hoped an infusion of Darius' Iranian blood would help him tolerate sunlight better? Ria shivered. Her own grandparents had come from India, so her skin was brown too. Would she have been next?

Or had she got it all the wrong way round? Had it

been Darius who had chosen Mr Rosenthal? Had he wanted to add that extra power to his existing charms? If so, he'd made a terrible mistake.

Afterwards, she saw how foolish she'd been to think she might save Darius! She'd run straight to Mr Johnson's office, had pleaded with the headteacher for the key to the cleaning cupboard, and please, please could he find the key to the inner cupboard? She'd seen the puzzlement in his eyes at her desperation.

Everyone around her had moved as though they were made of lead, so slowly it made her nerves scream! And yet what she'd seen, ultimately, had been only the very briefest glimpse before someone had pulled her away.

Brief but enough.

Darius had been kneeling on the floor in the gloom, bending over something. Once such a laughing, raucous, handsome boy, he was now pale and thin. Beyond him, a long box lay beneath the tiny window. On the side wall were scuffs marking out a quarter circle where the lid of the box had scraped open.

Ria stared. It was a coffin, and Mr Rosenthal was lying inside it on a bed of earth! For a moment, she thought he was dead. Then she saw his eyes flick open.

Darius straightened up. He turned. And Ria saw the thing that stayed in her mind forever after: a dark trickle at the corner of Darius' mouth and a pair of crimson droplets. They reminded her of tears, but they weren't tears, of course. They were on Darius' teeth. It was Mr Rosenthal's blood, collecting at the tips of a new vampire's fangs.

USB

Miss Torrington massaged her temples with the tips of her fingers. It was only 9:15, and already the day was going badly. She'd got stuck in roadworks this morning, arriving half an hour late only to find the coffee jar in the staffroom empty. The smell of coffee that hung in the air suggested she'd only just missed her caffeine hit. Now, she was having to face Year Five without it.

It had not been a good start to the day, and things hadn't improved when the children turned up. When she'd gone out to the playground to get the class in, Finley Owens had been mucking about in the line as usual. Today, he'd excelled himself by ripping the hood off Annabel Shenton's ridiculously expensive new coat. Miss Torrington's chest tightened at the thought of breaking the news to Mrs Shenton after school.

Back inside, Ivy-Louise Minson hadn't even tried to

battle her way through the children jostling in the cloakroom to hang up her own coat. Instead, she'd kept it on and started right away making up reasons why she needed to be sent home. Miss Torrington had insisted she take her coat off and come and sit down, and though the girl had done as she was told, she was now clutching her stomach and rolling her eyes. The same mystery illness afflicted her every morning between 8:48 and 8:52. Miss Torrington had tried to find out if there was something else going on, but to no avail.

Miss Torrington began to take the register, which Aiden Thomas took as his cue to try and climb out of the window. This was another daily occurrence, earlier than usual today because Aiden was making the most of Mrs Greenaway's absence. Miss Torrington assumed her T.A. had got stuck in the same traffic jam she had. Whatever the reason, she hadn't been on hand to pounce on Aiden the moment he slipped out of his seat.

Another disappointment followed hard on the heels of Miss Torrington pulling Aiden back into the classroom by *his* heels. Josh Ramirez hadn't handed in his homework and didn't seem able to offer an excuse for why not. In the grand scheme of things, it shouldn't matter. It was nothing, after all, to Aiden's escape attempts, or Finley's disruptive behaviour. It was nothing to trying to help Maisie, who was autistic, or keeping an eye on Ryan, who definitely had something a bit funny going on at home lately. It did matter, though, because kids like Josh Ramirez were the reason Miss Torrington had gone into teaching. On his good days, he was one of the reasons she stayed.

It wasn't that he was a model pupil. Far from it! When Josh had joined the school, rather out of the blue in the middle of Year Four, he'd been a tearaway and a trouble-maker, though that wasn't the reason he'd left Haltonbrook to come to St. Stephen's apparently.

Miss Torrington never had found out why he'd moved, but when he'd arrived in Year Five, she'd immediately warmed to him. There was a look in his eye that made you sure that underneath all the silly stuff, he was a decent kid. It was taking a while to find him, the decent kid, but Miss Torrington had been convinced she was getting somewhere. Only last week, he'd written the most amazing ghost story, so good she'd entered it for the competition the city library was running. She had high hopes he'd get somewhere with it, which was fantastic, given his reluctance to write anything at all a year ago.

She pressed a little harder with her fingertips and surveyed the class. She'd set the children to read quietly for fifteen minutes, partly to give herself a breather before they embarked on converting decimals to fractions, a lesson this class was absolutely going to hate! Now, she saw that Josh wasn't reading the book in front of him. It was open, but his eyes weren't moving across the page and he looked thoroughly miserable. That was so unlike him.

What on earth was going on? She hadn't told him off about the missing homework, although she was perplexed by his inability to explain where it was. He'd been so enthusiastic about the task – to make a model of a famous building. All week, he'd been talking about his Taj Mahal and all the features he'd included, inside and out. It wasn't a physical model, he said: one of his neighbours had let him go round and use their computer, and he'd constructed the whole thing in Minecraft. She was sure that was true. Even today, although he was subdued, he was adamant he'd

finished it. So where was it? Had he lost the files, and was too ashamed to say?

With a sigh, Miss Torrington turned her attention to the maths lesson, and put Josh and his homework out of her mind.

At lunchtime, while she was catching up with the art preparation she hadn't got done before school, Mrs Deacon burst in, bristling with importance.

"Josh Ramirez has run off!" the midday supervisor announced. "Went over the fence and off down the street. A right lick he was going!"

Miss Torrington frowned, still mentally among the Impressionists. "Are you sure it was him?" she asked vaguely.

Mrs Deacon launched into instant, full-throttle indignation. "Of course I'm sure!"

Miss Torrington blinked, regretting her question.

"Thirty five years I've been at this school!" The woman glowered. "I know every one of these kiddies, and most of their parents too!"

The teacher held up her hand in apology. "Of course, Mrs Deacon! I wasn't thinking. I'm sorry." She gave the supervisor her most winning smile. "I'll deal with it. If he isn't back by the end of lunch break, I'll phone his dad and see if he's turned up at home."

Mrs Deacon subsided a little. "I'll leave it with you, then," she said, her tone making clear what she thought of Miss Torrington's response.

Miss Torrington ignored this. "Thank you," she said, and returned pointedly to her preparation, wondering again what was going on with Josh.

As the bell rang, and the children came in, she scanned the heads for his wavy dark hair. He wasn't back. She took the register, calling his name anyway.

"Josh?" she repeated. "Does anyone know where Josh is?"

"I think he went home," Harry Carpenter said. "He said something about going to fetch his homework."

Miss Torrington looked up in surprise. "Why didn't he just tell me he'd forgotten it?" She finished the register. "Mrs Greenaway will help you start setting up for art," she said, and went to the office to phone Josh's dad.

Before she got there, however, Josh came racing

along the corridor red-faced and panting.

"Josh!" she exclaimed. "Where've you been?"

"Sorry, Miss!" he gasped.

"You know you shouldn't have climbed over the fence and left school like that! What were you thinking? It's against every rule!"

"I know." He caught his breath. "I'm sorry," he said again. "I really, really wanted to get my homework for you." With a sheepish smile, he held out a plastic bag. Miss Torrington took it and delved inside to find a USB stick. It was slightly damp in the bag. She wondered if there was an unpleasant smell, but decided not to comment just now. Maybe Josh had stepped in something nasty when he ran home. She would check in a moment if the smell didn't disappear.

"I hope it works." Josh was almost hopping with impatience. "Can we see?"

Miss Torrington turned back towards the classroom with him. This was more like the Josh she knew. Maybe everything was alright after all, though she would still have to speak to the headteacher about his escapade.

She went straight to her desk and sat down. "It's on here, then?" she said, holding up the USB key. He nodded. With one hand, Miss Torrington pushed back the paper landslide that had covered her keyboard, and with the other, tried to pull out the headphones that were plugged into the computer socket. The headphone cable started to rip away from the plug. Miss Torrington transferred Josh's USB stick to her teeth while she eased the headphone plug out very carefully with both hands. The USB was definitely damp, like the bag it had been in. And there was the smell again. Surely it couldn't be coming from the stick.

The headphones came loose. Miss Torrington took the USB from her mouth and plugged it in. The file menu popped up on the screen.

"Oh, Miss!" Josh's eyes gleamed. "It still works! It's okay! I didn't know if it would be."

She smiled at him, pleased by how excited he was. At least one thing had come right today!

"It seems fine," she said. "Did you lose it on the way to school, or forget it or something? Why didn't you just tell me?"

USB

"No, Miss." He dropped his gaze and looked uncomfortable. "I didn't forget, but I did sort of lose it. It's fine now, though," he went on hurriedly. "I cleaned it really well, honestly!"

Miss Torrington looked up, suddenly alert. She didn't think she'd closed her lips around the USB stick, yet she felt as if she could taste it on her tongue. "Tell me what happened, Josh," she said. Her stomach twisted inside her.

He peered out from beneath his dark mop of hair. His eyes were huge with worry. "It was Frodo, Miss," he whispered. The olive skin of his cheeks flushed a deep red. "It was too soon before school. I had to wait a bit, and then take him out. That's why I was gone a while."

Miss Torrington had a horrifying feeling that she knew what he was saying. She hoped fervently that she was wrong. "What do you mean? Who's Frodo?"

She had risen to her feet, she found. Her stomach surged. She had never been sick in front of a class before. That really would be the crowning disaster to a bad day!

"What exactly happened?" she asked. Her hands moved automatically towards her mouth, where the USB key

164

had been only moments ago.

"I'm sorry, Miss." Josh Ramirez stared at his teacher's computer screen. His voice faltered. "Frodo's our Dobermann, our dog. I'm really sorry, Miss Torrington. The dog ate my homework."

Leather

It was dark in the city library, or very nearly. Flickering lanterns on the tops of the bookcases lighted the way. Figures stood in the shadows, pointing.

Charlie made his way a little hesitantly towards the children's area. A couple of kids were there already, sitting on rugs in front of a chair lit by a small table lamp. Even though Charlie had recognised the silent figures as members of staff, the fact that they didn't speak and were dressed all in black made them seem unusually sinister. He looked around anxiously for Miss Burrows. He hadn't seen her so far, thank goodness! More than likely, she'd refused to be involved in an event like this.

It was quite late, after eight o'clock on a February night, and the library was closed to the public except for the winners and runners-up in the Children's Ghost Story Competition. Charlie was one of ten children who'd been invited to attend this special event. He hadn't been looking forward to it, and had even tried a few rather lame excuses. Since he'd never admitted to his parents why he'd stopped coming to the library on Saturday mornings, however, nothing he said made sense to them.

He found himself a spot on a nice thick rug and sat down. He always used to enjoy coming into town and spending time here while Dad did the shopping. These days, though, he ordered books online and got Dad to pick them up. It wasn't as enjoyable or as easy to choose as browsing along the shelves, but of course, since Miss Burrows had come, you couldn't browse anyway.

It was a real shame, Charlie thought. There were several librarians who worked here, most of them part time, some of them volunteers, and all of them very nice – except her. She'd taken over last year as Head of the Children's Section. The first time Charlie had visited after she'd arrived, he'd been taken aback to see her prowling around, eyes narrowed, watching over the shoulders of the children who were looking at books, and shushing anyone who made the slightest sound. It made the library an uncomfortable place to be. The old children's librarian had never minded a bit of chatter. She'd always been somewhere about the place, ready to help if you had a question, but otherwise busy reshelving books or working on the computer, not following you about!

Charlie hadn't been Miss Burrows' target on that visit. In fact, he'd survived several visits before it was his turn. That was her campaign he realised afterwards: to bully children out of coming to the library. She was picking them off, one by one, when their parents weren't looking.

On the last Saturday Charlie had come here, he knew from the moment he entered the children's area that he was in the glare of Miss Burrows' attention. Her eyes locked on

to him, like a hawk spying a mouse. He ignored her and headed over to the fiction for ten to twelve year olds, unwisely turning his back on her in order to browse.

Having decided against the first book he'd picked out, he started to put it back and nearly leapt out of his skin when her hand fell on his shoulder, like a claw.

"Don't touch books you don't want!" Miss Burrows hissed in his ear. "We don't want your filthy fingers all over them!" She snatched the book from him. "Show me your hands!"

Charlie held them out, palms up. They weren't too bad, given how grubby they could be.

"There!" Miss Burrows jabbed at an ink stain on one of his fingers. "You children have no respect for property!"

She flicked through the book. "See!" She thrust it in Charlie's face. "See what you did!"

Charlie looked. There was a pencil mark part way down one page.

"But I haven't got a pencil!" he protested. "And I only read the blurb and the first page! I didn't open it anywhere near the middle!"

"Keep. Your. Voice. Down!" Miss Burrows rasped. She seized another two books from the shelves and riffled through them. "There's this too! And this!" She slammed the books under his nose, so close he could hardly focus.

169

There was a slight tear in the page of one, and a smear of ketchup on the other. Charlie hadn't read either of them.

"And this one!" Miss Burrows' eyes glittered as she picked out a book she must have identified in advance. Charlie had taken this one out in the past, and its pages were wrinkled from getting wet. "You borrowed this book, didn't you? You returned it like this and didn't own up!"

"I didn't!" Charlie cried. "I have read it, but it was alright when I brought it back!"

"So you say!" Miss Burrows' face shrivelled up. "I'm taking you to the fines desk." She gripped his shoulder again. "They'll be able to call up your account. Then we'll see the list of all the books you've damaged."

Charlie scanned the library desperately. This was so unfair! He had never knowingly damaged a book. Was this what she'd been doing every time he'd seen her looming over another child?

Fortunately, Dad was just coming. "I can't do that now!" he said. "I've got to go."

Miss Burrows let go of him and whirled round, clearly suspecting a trick.

"Alright, Charlie?" Dad asked. "Found anything you want?"

Charlie glanced at Miss Burrows, wondering if she would march him to the fines desk right in front of Dad.

But she seemed to be melting into the background, tucking the books away she'd just picked out, like any ordinary librarian.

"Not today," Charlie told his father. "I might have a look at the catalogue later."

The last few kids arrived in the children's area now and sat down. Everyone waited expectantly.

Nothing happened. No-one came.

A door slammed somewhere in the building. For a second, there was complete silence, then two or three of the children began to giggle. A couple of the others started whispering. They must know each other. Charlie wished there was someone he knew in this group.

Another door slammed, this time closer. The giggling paused, then rose a little in pitch. Charlie found himself joining in without quite knowing why.

When the third door banged, really near this time, the laughter faltered. Charlie could feel invisible threads of tension knitting the air together. What if Miss Burrows was going to be part of this event? She could make a ghost story genuinely frightening!

The library was still. A clock struck, just once, not the

clock on the wall, but an old-fashioned timepiece. Its bell resonated through the building. Charlie peered about, but couldn't see where it had come from. Everyone seemed to be holding their breath.

There was a movement behind the children. Charlie swivelled round. A dark figure stepped out of a corner. Had someone been standing there all this time? A shiver rustled across Charlie's skin.

The man moved forward. Charlie was relieved to recognise him. This was one of the senior librarians, a tall, lean individual who always had a vague expression as he hurried around the library. He was dressed in black, with a high wing collar and a top hat, rather like a Victorian undertaker. The children shuffled aside to make a clear passage to the chair. As he reached it, the man flicked his coat tails and sat down, then removed the hat and put it on the table beside the lamp.

From inside his coat, he brought out a sheaf of papers. "Congratulations to you all," he said, in a rather mournful voice. "You ten children have written the best ghost stories of the many entries to the competition. You shall hear each one read aloud, and then we shall tell you a story of our own."

He began to read. Charlie hugged his arms round his knees and settled in to enjoy himself. All of the stories were quite good, and two in particular were much better than his, he thought. Nonetheless, his ghost story had won second place. It was strange hearing his own words read out, but he glowed with pride as the other children turned to smile at him when it finished.

The winning entry was by a boy called Josh. It was a story about a girl who'd choked to death on cat fur whilst try to eat the animal, and who'd rather unreasonably come back to haunt the cat's owners. Josh said he'd got the idea from something he'd seen in a newspaper. Charlie decided to look at the news more often in future. It would be worth it if this kind of thing was on there.

Having finished the ten stories, the librarian congratulated them all again, instructed them to wait where they were, put his hat back on, and stalked off into the gloom.

The clock struck again, three times. Quarter to nine. Charlie looked around, a little more relaxed than he'd been earlier. As long as Miss Burrows didn't turn up now, this would have been a good evening.

Someone pointed towards the far end of the library. A figure was advancing slowly through the shadows, dressed in old-fashioned clothes like the man. From the skirts brushing the floor, it was presumably a woman this time, but her face was hidden by a black veil. Her feet made no

173

sound on the polished floor so that she seemed to glide. In one hand, she carried an ancient book.

Charlie realised he was holding his breath again. As the woman drew close, he let it softly out. This was not Miss Burrows either; this woman was too small and slight.

She sat down in the chair and smoothed her skirt with hands gloved in black lace. She laid the leather-bound book in her lap, caressing the cover with her fingertips. After a pause, she said quietly, "Now, it is time for me to tell you a story."

Charlie expected her to open the book, but she didn't.

She cleared throat. "The story I'm going to tell you is a chilling one. It is also true: the true story of something quite terrible that happened long ago. It's the story of an extremely rare book that you can still see to this day in a museum in Bristol. If you've seen it already, you'll know what I'm talking about. It's a book you never forget."

She paused. Nobody spoke. Charlie found he was suddenly quite cold. Was there a draught somewhere, or had the woman somehow brought the cold with her?

"There was once a boy who loved a girl," she began, "but if you think this is going to be a love story, you are very much mistaken. The girl's name was Eliza. The boy's name was John. He was older than you are, but he wasn't yet eighteen."

She seemed to be looking at them all from behind her veil. "He loved Eliza with all his heart," she went on. "At least, that was what he told himself. She loved him too, for a time.

"But John was jealous. If Eliza smiled in the presence of a boy, he tasted bitterness in his mouth. If she talked of something she'd heard a man say, he seethed. Soon enough, when any man or boy so much as looked her way, John's hand flew up, ready to strike her. It was not long before Eliza couldn't bear it any more. She broke off their relationship."

The woman paused. She stroked the book in her lap.

"John was angry," she continued. "He could not stand it that Eliza should be happy without him. Night and day, he thought of nothing else. While he worked, he thought of ways to punish her for leaving him. While he slept, he dreamed of inflicting pain on her.

"He took to waiting outside Eliza's house. He followed her to the place where she worked, and lurked in doorways as she made her way home again in the evenings. He ambushed her in alleyways, and on the river path. He threatened her with his fists and his boots, and he took pleasure in sharpening the knife he carried, drawing it over his whetstone with silky sweeps as he shadowed her footsteps.

"One day, he met a man who offered him some oil of

vitriol, a kind of acid that burns whatever it touches. John bought it. If he could not have Eliza for himself, he swore he would use the acid to burn her skin, so that no man would ever look at her again. And he would blind her with it too, so that she would never look at any man again either."

The storyteller paused. Charlie edged forward.

"So he waited for her once more," the woman went on, "armed with this cruel weapon. As Eliza approached, he sprang out. But she was too quick for him, and knocked the flask from his hand. It shattered on the ground before the acid could burn her."

The woman's hands were still stroking the book. Why did she have it with her? Charlie wondered.

"Perhaps Eliza thought she had finally defeated John," the storyteller continued. "Perhaps she looked ahead to a better life without him. She did meet another man. But her happy ending was not to be.

"One January afternoon, John saw Eliza and her new lover walking by the river. Enraged, he seized a large stone and hurled it at her. It hit her head.

"At first, Eliza did not seem badly injured. After some days, however, the place where the stone had struck swelled with infection. A doctor at the infirmary decided to drill into Eliza's skull to relieve the pressure."

The woman stopped speaking. She was clutching the

176

book on her lap in both hands now.

"Two hundred years ago tonight," she said, "on the 17th of February 1821, Eliza died." She looked down and seemed to notice how tightly she was holding the book. She loosened her grip. Faint dents marked its soft cover where she had pressed her fingers into it.

The clock began to strike the hour. Nine.

"John was accused of Eliza's murder," the woman went on when the last chime had died away. "He was found guilty and hanged three days after his eighteenth birthday. His body was dissected in public, cut up in front of an audience, by the same doctor who had drilled into Eliza's skull. The doctor took John's skeleton home with him afterwards and kept it, with the noose still around its neck.

"Yet, this was still not quite the end for John. When his trial was over and he was dead, the notes from the trial were collected into a book. It was a thick book, and it needed a cover." The storyteller raised her head to gaze at the children from beneath her veil. Not one of them moved.

"The doctor who cut up John's body had first stripped it of its skin. He made the skin into leather. And so it was that the book was bound with the skin of the hanged man. It was a punishment to fit the crime."

There was total silence in the room. Then the woman stood up. She held her own book close to her chest. She had

177

not opened it all the time she was speaking.

Charlie had to ask. "Excuse me," he said. His voice sounded shockingly loud in the stillness. "Your book – the one you're holding – that's got a leather cover, hasn't it? Is that John's trial book?"

"Are you the ghost of Eliza?" asked one of the girls breathlessly.

The woman didn't reply. The question hung in the air. It should have been ridiculous to ask such a thing, Charlie thought. Yet it wasn't.

The air stirred behind the veil, either a gasp or a chuckle, Charlie couldn't tell which.

"This is quite a new book, in spite of its cover," the woman said at last, running her thumb across the end of the pages.

"What is it? Is it a story?"

She inclined her head. "It is. It's more than one story in fact. It's where I write down the stories I'm going to tell."

Another of the boys spoke up. "What's it called? Why didn't you read to us from it?"

Charlie was sure now that the woman was smiling. "It's called, 'Unlucky for Some'. I brought it to remind me of the story I wanted to tell you this evening. Goodnight, children."

Without another word, she stepped out of the group and glided away into the darkness of the library.

For almost a minute, the children stayed where they were. Then the nearest figure moved forward and pointed towards the exit. The children got up and began to make their way out. The two girls who knew each other whispered together, but nobody else spoke.

At the door, the senior librarian raised his top hat to them. "Congratulations again," he said. "The three winning stories will be printed in the newspaper next week." He bowed and ushered them out.

The following Saturday, Charlie decided to risk going to the library again. He really wanted to know who the mysterious storyteller had been and maybe ask to look at her strange book. He wasn't planning on borrowing any library books, though. He didn't want to get caught by Miss Burrows.

She wasn't there, however. Delighted, Charlie took

his time browsing in the children's area. Afterwards, he wandered through the adult library, looking for anyone who might have been the veiled woman. There was nobody slender enough.

At the information desk, the staff looked perplexed.

"I thought it was Mr Horton doing the readings," said one. "What did this lady look like? How old was she?"

Charlie frowned. Apart from her size, he had no idea.

"It might have been Lizzie," suggested another. "She's been working in the children's library since early December, but she left a week or two ago. Maybe she came back in to do the event with Mr Horton."

"What about Miss Burrows?" Charlie asked. "Is she off sick?"

The man behind the desk shook his head. "She hasn't been in since before Christmas. I don't know why. I'm not sure if she's expected back." He raised his eyebrows at Charlie. "Shame, eh?"

Charlie grinned.

Two days later, the national newspapers provided a definite answer on this point: a body had been found in a disused garage, where it had been undiscovered for two months or more. Police had identified the corpse as a Miss Heather Burrows, who had worked for the Devon Library Service for many years.

Miss Burrows had apparently last been seen shortly before Christmas in the company of a younger woman called Elizabeth Dossett, who had worked with her during the autumn, but also lived next door to Miss Burrows as a child growing up in Bristol. Police had been trying to trace Miss Dossett, without success. They were appealing for her to come forward urgently.

Charlie couldn't help a flush of relief to know he would never see Miss Burrows again. He also felt a secret satisfaction that something bad had happened to her.

As he read on, however, he began to be alarmed. There was one peculiar feature in the case, the newspaper reported: all of the skin had been removed from the dead woman's back. The police couldn't say whether there was any connection between the missing skin and the woman's death.

Charlie thought back to the veiled woman with her book of stories. Had he been in the presence of a murderer that evening? Had the storyteller been Elizabeth Dossett – Lizzie to her colleagues? Should he go to the police and tell them?

On the other hand, they were searching for her already. If there was a connection between the storyteller's book and Miss Burrows, they would find it.

He would let events take their course, Charlie decided. Apart from anything else, he didn't want to be the one to betray Lizzie. If she'd grown up living next door to Miss Burrows, she might have very good reasons for what she'd done.

One thing at least was clear to Charlie. If he was right about that book, then he'd been spectacularly wrong about Miss Burrows. He'd assumed she had refused to be involved in the ghost story event. In actual fact, she'd given everything just to be a part of it.

Also by Julia Edwards

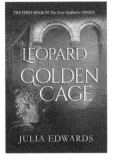

WHERE
WOULD
YOU
LIKE TO
GO?

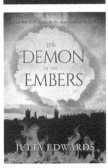

Who is Julia Edwards anyway?

Julia writes books (hopefully you'd realised that) and lives in Salisbury in the UK. Although the city was briefly famous for some Russians poisoning people, it is usually a lovely place to live. She is married to a kind but eccentric man who makes giant models of creepy-crawlies for fun. Julia has finally persuaded him to design these so they can live in the garden, which is a big improvement to the house. They have three sons aged seven, ten and thirteen who are mostly excellent humans, and who between them own two ferrets, two budgies and nine chickens. Julia feels this is definitely more than she signed up to.

Unlucky for Some is the first book in which Julia has revealed to her readers how nasty she really is. She previously wrote the much less vengeful *Scar Gatherer* series, seven time-travel adventures which allowed her to spend several years in parts of the past she's always wanted to visit. You can find out lots more about these books on the series website: *www.scargatherer.co.uk*.

Julia regularly visits schools, both in person and via Zoom, Teams and Google Classrooms. Find out more at *www.juliaedwardsbooks.com*.